Penguin Books
The Song o

H. E. Bates was born in 1905 at Rushden in Northamptonshire and was educated at Kettering Grammar School. He worked as a journalist and clerk on a local newspaper before publishing his first book, *The Two Sisters*, when he was twenty. In the next fifteen years he acquired a distinguished reputation for his stories about English country life. During the Second World War, he was a Squadron Leader in the R.A.F. and some of his stories of service life, *The Greatest People in the World* (1942), *How Sleep the Brave* (1943) and *The Face of England* (1953) were written under the pseudonym of 'Flying Officer X'. His subsequent novels of Burma, *The Purple Plain* and *The Jacaranda Tree*, and of India, *The Scarlet Sword*, stemmed directly or indirectly from his war experience in the Eastern theatre of war.

In 1958 his writing took a new direction with the appearance of *The Darling Buds of May*, the first of the popular Larkin family novels, which was followed by *A Breath of French Air*, *When the Green Woods Laugh* and *Oh! To Be in England* (1963). His autobiography appeared in three volumes, *The Vanished World* (1969), *The Blossoming World* (1971) and *The World in Ripeness* (1972). His last works included the novel, *The Triple Echo* (1971) and a collection of short stories, *The Song of the Wren* (1972). Perhaps one of his most famous works of fiction is the best-selling novel *Fair Stood the Wind for France* (1944). H. E. Bates also wrote miscellaneous works on gardening, essays on country life, several plays including *The Day of Glory* (1945); *The Modern Short Story* (1941) and a story for children, *The White Admiral* (1968). His works have been translated into 16 languages and a posthumous collection of his stories, *The Yellow Meads of Asphodel*, appeared in 1976.

H. E. Bates was awarded the C.B.E. in 1973 and died in January 1974. He was married in 1931 and had four children.

H. E. Bates

The Song of the Wren

Penguin Books

Penguin Books Ltd, Harmondsworth, Middlesex, England
Penguin Books, 625 Madison Avenue, New York, New York 10022, U.S.A.
Penguin Books Australia Ltd, Ringwood, Victoria, Australia
Penguin Books Canada Ltd, 2801 John Street, Markham, Ontario, Canada L3R 1B4
Penguin Books (N.Z.) Ltd, 182–190 Wairau Road, Auckland 10, New Zealand

First published by Michael Joseph 1972
Published in Penguin Books 1974
Reprinted 1974, 1976, 1979, 1982

Copyright © Evensford Productions Ltd, 1972
All rights reserved

Set, printed and bound in Great Britain by
Cox & Wyman Ltd, Reading
Set in Linotype Times

Except in the United States of America, this book is sold subject
to the condition that it shall not, by way of trade or otherwise, be lent,
re-sold, hired out, or otherwise circulated without the
publisher's prior consent in any form of binding or cover other than
that in which it is published and without a similar condition
including this condition being imposed on the subsequent purchaser

Contents

The Song of the Wren

The Song of the Wren

Miss Shuttleworth, moving with an air of delicate vacancy that also had something quite seriously studious about it, walked up and down the banks of the little stream running through the bottom of her garden, carefully distributing various sandwiches from a big blue plate.

Those of cucumber she placed on a large stone urn filled with budding violet petunias. Half a dozen of tomato she arranged about a clump of wild yellow irises growing at the water's edge. An assortment of anchovy paste, cream cheese, blackberry jam and Gentleman's Relish she set out at carefully measured intervals on the lawn that bordered the stream. When all had been distributed she stood back in a silence of contemplation that was almost reverent, surveying the result as if it were some fastidiously moulded work of art.

Finally she sat down on the lawn, legs carefully folded and tucked under her, and stared dreamily first at the sandwiches and then at the water sparkling in the warm June sunshine. Since she was wearing a floppy pink cotton dress and an even floppier pink straw hat from which straggling grey curls fell untidily to her shoulders, she looked not unlike a big, resting pink moth. Her intense blue eyes, large in concentration, gave her the impression of not belonging, quite, to this world.

Presently the eyes gave a sudden flutter of expectancy and then of positive, almost child-like delight.

'We're not alone, we're not alone,' she suddenly said in a sort of expanding whisper, 'we're not alone, we're not alone.'

Two pairs of birds, a male and female blue tit, then a male and female chaffinch, flew with a delicate flicker over the stream, the blue tits going straight for the cream cheese, the chaffinches for the Gentleman's Relish.

'Good, good, good,' Miss Shuttleworth said, again in a carefully expanded whisper, 'splendid, splendid. Clever creatures.'

Amazing how they knew, Miss Shuttleworth told herself. How did they know? Why was it the chaffinches always went, without fail, for the Gentleman's Relish and the blue tits for the cream cheese? Was it by some divine intuition or something of that sort? or perhaps a question of taste? However it was it struck her, always, as being little short of miraculous.

Half a minute later her wonder at these things was being enlarged to include a cock robin flying perkily over the clump of yellow irises.

'Don't fail me, don't fail me,' Miss Shuttleworth whispered, 'don't fail me.'

Before she had finished speaking the robin had settled among the tomato sandwiches. Now why always the tomato? Frequently Miss Shuttleworth was disposed to tell herself that it had something to do with coloration, the red of the tomato having some mysterious affinity with the red of the robin's breast. Could that be it? The fact that there was no answer merely served to increase her wonder.

It was still further increased when a bevy of sparrows descended in chattering disharmony on the anchovy paste, quarrelling greedily. She watched it all with excitement, well knowing that when the anchovy paste had all gone there would be a shrill rush for the blackberry jam. It was just like a properly organized meal, with the fish being followed by a sweet course. Naturally it didn't always work out quite like that, sparrows being what they were. Often they flouted the rules and raided the robin's tomato. Not that you could play fast and loose with cock robins for long. They were sharp enough to have their own back in no time.

Over on the far side of the stream a wren was singing his heart out in a willow tree, the notes pure silver. The wren too was a source of wonder. Why did the wren never, ever come to the sandwiches? Pure shyness? Indifference? She had asked herself these and a dozen other questions time and time again and had never come up, yet, with an answer.

For fully another three or four minutes she sat utterly absorbed in the brilliance of the wren's song, embalmed in a trance of fascination.

'Excuse me, madam.'

It was less the voice of a man speaking from somewhere behind her than the surprised fluttering of disturbed tits, sparrows, chaffinches and the cock robin that suddenly woke her out of her song-imprisoned trance.

'Oh! you startled me. Why – '

'I must apologize for the intrusion, madam. But I'm engaged in making a social survey and I wondered if you would mind answering a few questions.'

'A survey? About what? Why me? Is it something personal?'

'It's a general survey on a great variety of subjects.'

'What is the point of it?'

'Eventually all the answers will go into a computer and the results will, I hope, become a book.'

Miss Shuttleworth could think of nothing to say. She thought the man was perhaps thirty-five. His large, black-rimmed glasses did not conceal the deadly seriousness of his eyes.

He now proceeded to sit down on the grass, at the same time producing from an attaché case a thick blue notebook, several sheets of foolscap paper and a ballpoint pen. A consultation of the sheets of foolscap kept him utterly quiet for fully a minute. during which the tits and sparrows began to fly back.

'What an extraordinary, amazing, astonishing thing. The tits have gone for the Gentleman's Relish. They've never, ever done that before.'

'I'm sorry, madam. What did you say?'

'I said the tits have gone for the Gentleman's Relish. Why, I wonder? I suppose they could have sensed the presence of a stranger.'

'I'm sorry, madam. I don't think I quite understand what you're talking about.'

'My birds. I allot them certain sandwiches every day. They always go for the same ones. They sort of do it according to the Laws of the Medes and Persians.'

'Oh! they do, do they?'

The man stared hard, eyes big and serious with disbelief, into the sun. This caused him suddenly to sneeze loudly and violently and Miss Shuttleworth said:

'Blessings upon you. Blessings upon you.'

'And what exactly does that mean?'

'Oh! one always says that, doesn't one? I even say it to the birds. Starlings give a sort of sneeze sometimes. Of course they're great imitators, starlings. I suppose they might well pick it up from us humans. The sneezing, I mean.'

In silent disbelief the man stared at his notebook, momentarily lost in a trance of his own. Coming out of it at last he said:

'Oh! by the way, my name's Adamson. Would you mind if I asked you a few questions now?'

'Oh! ask away. For the life of me I can't think what I can do to help, I mean, why me?'

'It isn't merely a question of one person. It's a complex cross-section and sub-sections of views on an infinity of subjects. From them the computer will build up a picture. For instance what do you think about the Common Market?'

'What market?'

'The Common Market. What are your views on that?'

Miss Shuttleworth, eyes slowly revolving in order to catch a possible glimpse of birds coming back, was obliged to confess she had never heard of the Common Market.

'Oh! but you must have. After all it's been top news in all the papers for weeks.'

Miss Shuttleworth was also obliged to confess that she never read newspapers.

'But you must have heard it mentioned on radio and television. Or both.'

Miss Shuttleworth was now obliged to confess that she had neither radio nor television, a confession that caused Mr Adamson to make a protracted entry in his notebook.

'Well, what about space? What are your views on that? You see any purpose, for instance, in further exploration?'

'I often wonder what birds think about when they're flying about in space. Do you suppose birds think?'

'No. Not in the sense that we do.'

'But I do, you see, I do. I mean the sandwiches, for instance. They must think about those, you see. It must be conscious thought that makes them do what they do.'

'Oh? Well, we'll leave space for the moment. What about the permissive society?'

'The what society?'

'The permissive society.'

'Is it for the prevention of something? I never heard of it. Can one join?'

'Not exactly. It's a sort of breaking down of rigid rules and pre-accepted social behaviour and moral attitudes and so on. I mean should the young indulge in pre-marital intercourse for instance?'

'Well, they always have, haven't they?'

'What I mean is that there seems to be an entirely new manifestation of it. Do you approve of that or not?'

'Birds don't get married, do they? Why should humans simply in order to propagate the species?'

'I'm sorry, but I don't think you quite get my point.'

'Well, what is the point?'

'A whole new pattern of social behaviour is emerging and sex would seem to be the mainspring of it. Have you any views on that?'

'Oh! just hark at that wren. If that isn't sheer divinity I'd like to know what is. Exquisite, so exquisite. Ethereal, in fact, ethereal.'

'All right, divinity. What are your views on religion?'

'Which one?'

'Accepted religion. Organized. The church.'

'Would you be surprised if I told you I worshipped birds?'

'I'm very fond of birds myself. But they've nothing to do with religion.'

'But they have, they have. They *are* religion. That wren is just as surely an apostle as any who fished the Sea of Galilee.'

'Well, we'll leave religion. What about life after death?'

'Now I've a question for you. I was asked it by a small boy the other day. He comes into the garden sometimes with his fishing rod and a bent pin and a worm and tries to catch fish in the stream. And the other day as he was putting a worm on his hook he asked me if I thought a worm had a heart? Now there's a question for your computer.'

'Possibly. But hardly one of much social significance.'

'I disagree. I disagree. Are not two sparrows sold for a farthing?'

'I'm sorry, but I think we're straying from the main purpose.'

'Surely not. The question of whether a worm has a heart or whether two sparrows are sold for a farthing is just as significant as your permissive market.'

'Society.'

'But society is a market. In which, if I'm not much mistaken, sex is sold.'

'Yes, yes. Do you mind if I make a note?' With serious concentration Mr Adamson made a note in his big blue book. After doing so he took off his spectacles, breathed on them and then polished the lenses with his handkerchief. As he did this his eyes looked remarkably, even innocently, naked.

He then turned to his sheets of foolscap. On them were a number of questions for which he still sought answers: abortion, the multi-racial society, immigration, the pill and whether sex should be taught in schools, but suddenly, before he could ask Miss Shuttleworth for her views on such matters, she leapt to her feet as if startled.

'Good gracious, I hear the church clock striking twelve! I must go and feed the hens. They'll never forgive me if I forget them. I have one that talks, you know.'

'Indeed.'

'In her own language of course, though I understand it perfectly – as in fact I should by now. I've had her donkey's years. Of course people are inclined to laugh when I say I hold conversations with a hen, but after all people talk to their dogs, don't they? And anyway I'd rather talk to my Biddy than to a lot of people I could name. You will forgive me if I go?'

'Of course. Thank you for giving me so much of your time.'

'Why don't you come too?' Miss Shuttleworth actually

laughed, her voice pitched excitedly high. 'You could ask Biddy a question for your computer. For instance what it feels like to go cluck.'

'Cluck?'

'Broody. Cluck is the local word. Sometimes I feel like going cluck myself. Do you ever?'

Mr Adamson refrained from saying whether he himself ever felt like going cluck and proceeded to pack his notebook and papers into his attaché case.

'I must fly!' Miss Shuttleworth said. 'Fly. Do excuse me. Good-bye.'

Miss Shuttleworth seemed positively to take to the air as she swept across the lawn, looking more than ever like a huge floppy pink moth.

For a few seconds Mr Adamson stared after her. 'Mad. Quite, quite mad,' he told himself. 'Has a worm got a heart? Do birds think? Are not two sparrows sold for a farthing? Really, sometimes one really doesn't know. One really wonders.'

Across the stream the wren again poured out its ethereal cadence of song, all sweetness on the warm June air, but Mr Adamson, pausing to extract his notebook from the attaché case and record in it a quick, earnest note, appeared not to be listening.

There were clearly things of greater importance on his mind.

The Dam

The Dam

Sometimes, even in September, the lightest sprinkle of fresh snow, like a crusting of white sugar across a cake top, lay on the mountains above the lake. Well before noon the heat of the sun had melted it away.

At the foot of the hotel garden, parallel with the lakeside, ran a pergola of iron grey rock on which grew old and twisted grape vines. The grapes, on their dark muscular branches, everywhere falling off from sheer ripeness, were small, purple black and of a wonderfully aromatic sweetness.

Every morning, with a punctuality so regimented that it was as if she were under military orders, a tall German woman of fifty or so came and sat in the shade of the pergola with a sketching pad, arriving on the stroke of ten o'clock and leaving as a church bell up the mountainside chimed for noon. Upright, stiffish, thick hair blonde almost to a point of illumination, she was, with her pale high cheekbones and Nordically cold blue eyes, strikingly handsome rather than beautiful.

Her first act before taking up her pencil to begin sketching was to gather herself a bunch of grapes. These she then ate slowly, one by one, also at regimented intervals, skin, pips and all, her full lips slowly protruding and then sucking inward almost as in an act of kissing.

It was this act, more than anything else about her, that fascinated George Graham as he sat in the garden, some distance away, trying to read. The sensuous nature of the lips seemed not to belong to the cold statuary of the rest of her face. She seemed, he thought, to be two distinct persons, locked in fascinating disturbing contradiction.

For four mornings the sun had the brilliance and heat of full summer. The surface of the lake had a sparkling glassiness that almost hurt the eyes. On the fifth day clouds started to gather early on the highest crests of the mountains and well before noon a gusty coolish breeze was blowing sharply down the lake from the west.

When a sharper sweep of wind suddenly blew several sheets of sketching paper across the hotel lawn George Graham leapt up from his chair and started to gather them up.

When he took them across the lawn to her he began to say something about the inadequate nature of his German when she interrupted with a smile that came only from her lips, stained now to a deep purple, and not in the remotest degree from her eyes:

'That is most kind of you,' she said in English. 'I am very grateful.'

'The breeze,' he said, 'is rather strong this morning.'

'Yes. I feel rain in the air. I hope the weather is not about to break.'

'I don't think so. Usually the weather remains good here until at least November.'

'So this is evidently not your first visit?'

'No. I have been twice before.'

'So? Well, it is very beautiful.'

During this formal, even slightly stiff exchange he found himself increasingly surprised and fascinated by what he saw on her sketching pad.

She was drawing not the landscape of cream-white Italian villas, black pencil-straight cypresses and the white and scarlet sails of a few yachts tacking in the breeze across the lake, but the profile of a girl. It too was formal. In its rather wooden way it might have been a portrait of herself, twenty-five years younger.

'Please don't look too much at my work. I am not good. It is merely to pass the time.'

'I am fascinated,' he said. 'I mean because you are sketching something that isn't there.'

'I am not good at landscapes, you see. They rather bore me.'

'May I ask who is the girl?'

20

'My daughter.'

'Of course I can't tell if the likeness is good, but she looks attractive.'

She put a grape into her mouth, went through the sensuous act of slowly eating it, at the same time regarding him with eyes completely cold.

'You find it so?'

'I was going to say that she looks a good deal like you.'

'Perhaps the compliment is a doubtful one.'

'I assure you it wasn't intended to be.'

Suddenly there was no sun. The breeze blew quite cold. She glanced at her wrist watch.

'I find it not too pleasant any more.'

'No. It's one of those days when you are glad you have a car. Did you bring a car?'

'No. I flew.'

'I think I shall have a drive somewhere this afternoon. Have you seen the new big dam they have built up the valley? It's really quite magnificent.'

'No. I have not seen it.'

'You really should. Perhaps you would care to come and see it with me this afternoon?'

She put another grape into her mouth, again went through the sensuous, disturbing act of eating it and then said, rather hesitantly he thought:

'That is very kind of you.'

'Does that mean that you would like to come?'

'I will come. Yes.'

'Ah! but I said would you *like* to come?'

A spasm of sunlight broke through the cloud and illuminated the lake, the cream-white villas and, through a narrow break in the arbour of vines, her face. For a brief moment or two he could have sworn that there was the slightest flush under her cheekbones.

'Yes,' she said, 'I would like to come.'

*

'There isn't much water coming down at this time of year,' George Graham said. 'In fact almost none at all.'

He had parked his car at a point where the full dry bowl of the dam stretched across the valley between gigantic limestone fists of rock. On all sides stiff blackish pines, interspersed with many Spanish chestnuts, their leaves already partly brown, covered the almost perpendicular mountain sides. The dam had the appearance of a great arena, dramatic but deserted, waiting for some sensational act to begin.

By now the wind of the morning had dropped. The afternoon air had about it a tight uncanny quietness. By contrast the voices of George Graham and the German woman seemed extraordinarily magnified.

'Shall we move on?' she suddenly said. 'I can hardly bear to look down.'

'Yes. I am not all that fond of heights myself.'

'And yet you come to look at the dam.'

'It fascinates me.'

They walked back to the car. They got in and the German woman said:

'Where does the road lead to?'

'Nowhere. There's a village a few miles up the valley and shortly afterwards the road stops. I'm glad to see you brought a coat. It sometimes gets very cold at the top of the valley.'

He started the car and then began to drive up the new, smooth, well-engineered road.

'Anyway, if it gets cold we can always go into the *trattoria* and have hot coffee,' he said. 'They have very good mountain cheese there too. And marvellous bread. The best bread you ever tasted.'

Now and then an angler came into view, wading in the mountain stream between whitish, water-smoothed slabs of rock.

'They have wonderful trout too. Quite pink. Like salmon.'

Soon the conversation between them died from sheer formality. For some minutes he searched for a new line of talk and at last said:

'By the way, how old is your daughter?'

'Trüdi is twenty-five.'

'She looks rather older than that in your picture.'

'Perhaps that is my fault.'

'Incidentally I don't know your name.'

'Gerda. Gerda Hauptman.'

'Mine's George Graham. I must say I still think you and your daughter are very much alike.'

'So? Well, you will be able to judge for yourself next week when she arrives. That is to say if you are still here.'

'Yes. I shall be here.'

Twenty minutes later he was parking the car in the centre of the last village at the head of the valley.

'What would you like to do?' he said. 'Have something to drink? Or walk? It's possible to walk for quite a way yet.'

'I prefer to walk I think.'

As they started to walk he suddenly noticed that she had left her coat in the back of the car.

'You've left your coat. You'll need it I'm afraid.'

'Oh! no. I never feel the cold.'

She was wearing a dark green woollen sweater with a dark brown skirt. In the sweater her bust stood out strong and handsome.

For twenty minutes or so they walked steeply upward on a dry stony path, by the river that was now no more than a gentle, limpid trickle. By this time the afternoon, far from becoming the cold one he had predicted, had become sunny and, in the clarified air, quite hot.

'Shall we sit down?' he said. 'There's a rock there that's almost like a seat.'

'Yes. Shall we do that? You see, after all it's quite hot in the sun.'

Sitting on the rock she adopted a pose of embracing her legs about the knees. The clean profile of her face and the blonde mass of her head had more than ever a look of being intensely luminous. He felt himself stirred by this and said:

'So you react to heights very much as I do.'

'When I was younger I did a good deal of mountain climbing but I never quite got over that odd feeling of – '

'They say that mountain climbing is really a substitute for something else.'

'So? For what?'

'In the case of a man the mountain is a woman.'

She laughed full throatedly. 'Oh! that's a ridiculous idea.'

'I don't think so. For instance – '

'Yes?'

'For instance when I sit here with you it's quite different from – '

He suddenly broke off and put his hands on her shoulders and then firmly on her strong fleshy upper arms. In return she made no movement. She simply held him fully but coldly with her eyes.

When he finally leaned forward in an attempt to kiss her she held her face averted.

'Do you always regard women so freely?'

'I find you very attractive.'

'Don't you see I am wearing a wedding ring?'

'That doesn't necessarily mean – '

'You have no need to be anxious about that matter. My husband is dead.'

He still held her by the upper arms and she in turn still held her face averted.

'Tell me something,' he said. 'You're still young and very attractive. Doesn't the fact of no longer – I mean that there's no love – '

'It is surely very natural.'

'Then let me kiss you.'

She suddenly stood up, smoothing her skirt into place with her hands.

'Not today. I am sorry. But not today.'

Twice during the next four days they walked up the same mountain path. Twice on the way back they stopped at the village *trattoria* to eat great hunks of rough-crusted bread and a soft sharp local cheese and drink a few glasses of dark red wine. On the second of these afternoons she suddenly said:

'Well, Trüdi will be here tomorrow. That is if she doesn't miss the train.'

'Have you any reason to think she might miss the train?'

'It would be exactly like her. She will probably forget to change at Domodossola and go on to Milan.'

'I would drive you to Domodossola to meet her. I have nothing else to do.'

'That would be pampering her.'

Whenever she spoke of Trüdi her entire manner seemed to change. She spoke with an impatience slightly touched with contempt. As they finished the last of the bread and cheese and wine that afternoon she even went so far as to say:

'Oh! let us change the subject. The young are so possessive nowadays. Don't you think?'

He had no idea what to make of this remark and made no answer.

On the way back down the valley her manner underwent another change. She seemed to exude a sort of brooding warmth. She had, he thought, never seemed so feminine. The habitual coldness of the pale blue eyes was actually replaced by tenderness.

She then drew his attention to a curious and ancient bridge, built of stone and in the shape of a high narrow bow, that spanned the river two kilometres above the dam.

'I have always wanted to see what there is on the other side of that strange little bridge,' she said.

'Well, then, we must go and see.'

He stopped the car. They got out and walked across the bridge, stopping half-way for the briefest interval to look at and listen to the narrow white torrent of water squirming swiftly through the marble-like rocks below.

On the other side the path disappeared into a steep stretch of woodland. Dark regiments of pines shut out the sun. Fifty yards up the path stood a small open wooden shack and he said:

'Well, now we know what's here.'

'Yes. It looks as if it were built for woodmen.'

They sat on the seat inside the hut. Again he could strongly sense the new warmth in her, now so tangible that he actually felt capable of touching it with his hands. In turn she looked at him for some moments with unbelievable softness, and he suddenly felt moved to kiss her.

Before accepting his kiss she said simply:

'Your touch is very warm.'

After he had kissed her at considerable length she gently broke away and said:

'I thought a great deal about what you said the other day.'

'About love?'

'About love.'

'It was true?'

'It was true. Last night I couldn't sleep and I went out and sat on my balcony. It was very warm. There is a big palm tree just under the window and they've put a light in it. The palm is in flower and under the light the flowers look like – oh! rather like a shower of fireworks.'

He sat completely entranced by this quite new vision of her, so opposite to the former stiff, cold Teutonic, regimented air.

'That was a very beautiful kiss you gave me just now,' she said. 'Why are you waiting so long before you give me another?'

Again he kissed her. Far below, the coursing of the river was like an echo of his own heart racing against hers.

Next morning they drove to Domodossola to meet the train. The road, going through remote villages, through countryside that seemed forgotten, was ill-paved and in places grass-grown and treacherous.

It seemed almost as if all this might have been responsible, in her, for another change of mood. A grey gloom had settled on her. The warm intensity of her manner during the previous afternoon had given place to something curiously cryptic and dry.

'Why we are doing this I can't imagine. She is probably still in Munich.'

'Well, we shall soon know.'

'She forgets as easily as other people breathe. She will forget her own name one of these days.'

As they went through the next village it occurred to him that possibly a glass of wine, or perhaps a cognac might do something to change her mood. When he suggested it she simply replied:

'No. It might mean that we ourselves would miss the train.'

They drove on for another five kilometres or so before she spoke again.

'I ought to warn you,' she said, 'that she doesn't speak very good English.'

'Not like you. Where did you learn yours?'

'I had a good teacher.'

At the station they waited a mere three minutes before the train came down from the direction of the Simplon. And suddenly, as it drew to a standstill, he half-wished he had never come. In turn she stood nervously locking and unlocking her fingers.

There then emerged from the train a figure that astonished him. Dressed in a light peach-coloured costume and carrying a small blue suitcase, she walked along the platform with poise, gracefully. He had prepared himself for something awkward, even gawky, a sort of gauche schoolmistress. Now she was revealed as a slightly taller, much slimmer, much less Teutonic figure than her mother. Her hair was several shades deeper than that of her mother's too.

Then an odd scene occurred. The two women greeted each other with such coldness, with neither handshake nor kiss, that there was a tangible feeling of animosity in the air.

'This is Trüdi, Mr Graham.'

'I am pleased to know you, Mr Graham,' the girl said.

'Good morning,' he said. 'May I take your suitcase? We have a car.'

'That is most kind of you.'

The excellence of the English was his second cause for astonishment. He took her suitcase. The warmth with which she smiled at him in return amazed him yet a third time.

He put the suitcase into the boot of the car and then held open one of the rear doors so that she could get in. Instead of doing so she paused and said:

'Do you mind if I sit in the front? I'm inclined to get car sickness if I sit in the back.'

'By all means.'

The next thing he knew was an almost violent slam of the rear door as her mother got into the back of the car.

He then held open the front door and the girl got in. He too got in, started the car and then said:

'That back road is positively ghastly. I really don't think I could face it again. Shall we go back by the lakeside? What do you say, Mrs Hauptman?'

'As you wish.'

At this point the girl gave him a sudden strange look of disbelief. Completely mystified, he also completely failed to understand it until some time afterwards.

Meanwhile, as they drove down through woods of acacia to the lakeside, she continued to astonish him. She chatted quickly, even volubly, perfectly at ease. The surface of the lake sparkled in the midday sun. Oleanders, cream and pink and white, were still in prolific bloom. Over and over again she said how beautiful it all was but from Mrs Hauptman there came not even a solitary syllable of any kind.

As the three of them got out of the car at the hotel he said:

'Perhaps you would both care to join me in a drink before lunch?'

'Not for me,' Mrs Hauptman said. 'I am rather tired.'

The girl said: 'Lovely idea. I'm dying of thirst.'

Without another word Mrs Hauptman left them and presently he and the girl were sitting on the hotel terrace. He raised his hand to summon a waiter and said:

'What will you drink, Miss Hauptman?'

'Oh! something long and cool.'

'Cinzano with ice and soda perhaps?'

'That will do splendidly. Incidentally my name is not Hauptman.'

He was too astonished, this time, to speak.

'It is Johnson. You see,' she said, 'I am half English.'

*

He pondered on the mysterious nature of all this during lunch, which he ate on the terrace, alone. The girl too sat alone. Mrs Hauptman did not appear.

Having finished his lunch he went over to the girl and said:

'I wondered perhaps if you'd care to take coffee with me? We could have it in the garden. It's rather nice down there.'

'Thank you. Yes.'

In the garden he said:

'Shade or sun?'

'I think shade. It's really quite hot now.'

When the coffee finally came the waiter put it on one of the stone tables under the pergola of vines. Many fallen grapes lay on the ground, on the table and on the stone seats, like so many small black-purple birds' eggs.

She picked up one of these, pressed it to her lips and proceeded to go through precisely the same act of pressing it to her lips as in an act of kissing, exactly like her mother, and then eating it, skin, flesh, pips and all. The sight of her doing this woke in him an extraordinary warm sense of intimacy and she said:

'They are wonderfully sweet. And sort of perfumed.'

'Yes,' he said and her lips were stained with purple.

He found it difficult to re-open the subject of her name and at last said instead:

'Your mother didn't appear at lunch, I noticed. I hope she isn't unwell.'

'I shouldn't worry about her,' she said and in her voice there was a note of indifference that bordered closely on contempt.

Then, after half an hour of talking trivialities and sipping coffee, she suddenly said:

'I think after all I'll lie in the sun. It seems a pity not to enjoy it. Will you excuse me while I go and put on my sun-suit?'

She went into the hotel and came back after ten minutes or so wearing a pure white two-piece sun-suit and then proceeded to lie in one of the long chairs the hotel provided, face uplifted to the sun.

The perfection of her figure captivated him deeply. Her breasts were taut and deep. Her bare navel was like some small exquisite snail shell. Her entire body was tanned to a golden even brown.

'You are marvellously tanned,' he said.

'Oh! I work hard at it.'

'So you should. A figure like that deserves it.'

'Thank you. I'm glad you approve.'

She shut her eyes. Then after lying in that supine position for twenty minutes or so she suddenly sat up, produced a bottle of sun lotion from her handbag and began to oil her arms, legs and thighs until they glistened in the sun.

'Now I must cook on the other side,' she said. 'Would you care to do my back?'

'Nothing would give me greater pleasure.'

Slowly, caressively, he oiled her back and shoulders and then the backs of her thighs. At the first touch of his palm on her thighs she gave a great sigh, half turned her face and gave him a long slow look that was itself caressive.

'I hope I'm not bungling it,' he said.

'You are quite expert.'

'Thank you.'

'And very gentle.'

He swept his hand down the full stretch of her right leg and she responded by saying:

'It's really very nice finding someone like you here. The last time I was here the place was full of stuffed dummies. All Germans. All heel-clicking and bowing and on parade and bridge-playing – bah!'

'Oh! you have been before? Well, they are still here.'

'What a difference there is between the English and the Germans.'

'A million miles.'

'Do you find anything Germanic in me?'

'Not a shred. To me you look pure English.'

'I can't tell you how grateful I am for that.'

It seemed a good moment in which to renew the subject of her mother and he said:

'I don't quite understand about your mother. Why is her name Hauptman and yours – '

'She and my father were not married.'

'I am sorry I embarrassed you.'

'Oh! it doesn't embarrass me.'

'But your name should still be Hauptman.'

'I prefer my father's name.'

Again he was mystified and again decided to drop the subject. She had different views:

'He was a journalist. He worked in Munich before the war. And then – '

She broke off and slowly turned her entire body and lay on her back.

'What were you going to say?' he said.

'Oh! she killed him. That's all.'

'She *what*?'

'You can put a little more on my front now if you like,' she said and again she gave him a long caressive smile. 'Have you been flirting with her? My mother I mean.'

'I think we've been quite good friends.'

'She's a widow, don't forget. Widows have needs.'

He laughed. 'For a moment I thought you said weeds.'

'No, no. Deep, deep needs.'

He brushed his hands across her shoulders and then centrally across her body. The gold-brown glistening of her skin in the full brilliance of the afternoon sun captivated him to such an extent that he was totally unprepared for the shadow that suddenly fell across it.

He turned his head to see Mrs Hauptman standing full in the path of the sun.

'I'm sorry to interrupt your labours, but you promised to take me for a drive at four o'clock.'

Suddenly he knew that he was in a trap. He was impotent either to argue or deny. To his intense annoyance Mrs Hauptman actually smiled and said:

'I've been waiting on the terrace. It's already ten past now.'

'I'll just wash my hands.'

Half savagely, baffled, without another word, he strode into the hotel.

*

As he and Mrs Hauptman drove along the opposite shore of the lake it was his turn to be wrapped into a withdrawn, darkly stubborn mood.

'You are very quiet this afternoon.'

'There are times when I like being quiet.'

Mrs Hauptman gave a short provocative laugh.

'What has that daughter of mine been saying to you? I should have warned you that she is a great liar.'

'You might also have warned me that she is very attractive.'

'It took you no time at all to discover that.'

'Naturally.'

'She is an impossible man-hunter. She has been in love with fifty men – well, I say in love – '

The scorn in her voice was sharp and acid.

'Would you care to stop for some tea?' he said.

No, she wouldn't, she said. But there was another, smaller lake some few kilometres farther on – she had seen it once before and would now like to see it once again.

It took them another twenty minutes to drive to the smaller lake. Sheltered by miniature hills everywhere dotted about with dark candles of cypress it had a depth of translucent blue as clear as glass in the warm afternoon sun.

After he had stopped the car by the lakeside Mrs Hauptman's first act was to take off the white cardigan she was wearing. Underneath it she had on a blouse of daffodil yellow silk and it seemed not without significance that it was cut rather low at the neck.

'Yes, she leaves a trail of broken hearts behind her wherever she goes, that girl.'

'It isn't my intention to fall in love with her, if that's what you're getting at.'

'Love? She doesn't know the meaning of the word.'

She rested her head on the car seat and held him for fully a minute in a long earnest gaze.

'You haven't kissed me today.'

He proceeded to kiss her. There was no sort of ardour in it and she was quick to notice it and drew her lips away.

'You are a different person today,' she said.

'One can't always be the same.'

She slipped a little lower into the car seat, so that the upper curve of her breasts was revealed.

'You caressed my breasts the other day. When a woman allows that she naturally – '

She broke off and suddenly he was provoked into an extraordinary sensation. It was compound of anger and a great desire to hurt her. With an almost violent gesture he kissed her again, at the same time unbuttoning her blouse.

The instant his hands touched her body he was aware of yet another extraordinary sensation. It was that he was back on the other lakeside, with the girl, and that it was she he was kissing and not her mother.

For the next two days he was never alone with the girl. Whenever he chanced to meet her on the hotel terrace, in the garden or in the public rooms Mrs Hauptman, as if by some uncanny instinct, appeared too.

On the evening of the third day he went out, about ten o'clock, to post some letters. The night was exceptionally warm and balmy, the air full of the heavy perfume of some tree whose flowers were invisible in the darkness.

'I thought you'd completely deserted me.'

The voice of the girl was not much more than a whisper. She was sitting on a wooden seat at the very edge of the lakeside. A few rowing boats were moored below, utterly motionless in the windless air.

'It's difficult to escape from a glass case,' he said.

'Except by breaking the glass.'

He sat down on the seat beside her. The air was so warm that she had slipped off her white woollen cardigan and draped it round her shoulders.

'I wanted to ask you something,' he said.

'About what?'

'You said an extraordinary thing about your mother that day I first met you. That she killed your father.'

'Oh! I didn't mean that she shot him or anything so dramatic. It was far more subtle than that.'

'I wanted to ask you something else too. If you hate her so much why do you come all the way from Munich to be with her?'

'It's more satisfying to be near the object you hate.'

He found it hard to make anything of this remark and was silent for some time. Then he said:

'Tell me about your father.'

'Let's walk, shall we?'

They walked for perhaps a quarter of a mile along the lake until eventually they came to another seat, under a huge flowerless magnolia tree. The great thick-leaved branches of this tree acted as a dark barrier, shutting out all sound except the minutest lappings of infinitely small waves breaking on the stones of the lake shore below. It also hid all but a few low stars, scattered like golden seed in the gaps between the mountains.

'Perhaps you'd rather not talk about your father.'

'I think I told you he was a journalist. Working for a London paper. It seems he was very gay. But then, in the thirties, all Munich was very gay. Nobody did much work. They drank much wine, much beer and talked a lot in cafés. Nobody had much money. They didn't need much. There's a story about my father that one Christmas he asked to borrow ten marks from his landlady. She lent it to him and he immediately gave her back five marks as a Christmas present. Now you get what sort of man he was.'

'Attractive to your mother, of course, and Herr Hauptman?'

'Professor Hauptman. Bio-chemical research. An eighteen-hours-a-day man, worshipping at the laboratory altar. Could you blame her, after all?'

'Hardly. The gay, debonair, wine-bibbing young journalist. Café society.'

'Wrong. He had a pair of ears sharper than a fox's. He wasn't merely a good journalist. He had a knack of listening to history before it was made.'

Again he had to confess that he didn't quite understand.

'He had a thousand contacts. His ears did the rest. Result – he was able to prophesy, step by step, the Hitler pattern. The Saar, Sudetenland, Danzig, Czechoslovakia, Austria, France – even England. It all went home to London in dispatches.'

'And not a damn soul took the slightest notice.'

'How did you know?'

'Not the first time it's happened, I suppose. There's a fire in the basement and somebody is having a cocktail party upstairs. "Isn't that smoke I smell?" someone says. "Smoke, my foot. It's the gin burning your tonsils." Nero all over again.'

He laughed. She was quiet.

'Well,' he said, 'what else?'

'He predicted the start of war almost to the day. Almost to the hour.'

'And powerless to do anything about it.'

'Wrong again. He decided to go back to London and say, plain and straight as he could, what he'd merely written before. That was in August 1939. And then all hell broke loose.'

'In August? I thought it didn't break until September.'

'My mother found she was pregnant.'

It was his turn to be quiet now. In a long silence he listened to the small waves breaking gently on the shore below, like low voices in pointless conversation.

At last she said: 'You've heard of feminine intuition?'

'Just as I've heard of bread-and-butter.'

'There was an infernal row. A hideous quarrel. Almost murderous. He was determined to go to London before it was too late. She was equally determined he shouldn't.'

'Feminine intuition. She had a hunch he wouldn't come back.'

'It's naturally in any woman's mind. In such circumstances.'

'She could have gone with him.'

'And desert the Third Reich? Mr Graham, you don't seem to know much of what substitute there was for blood in German veins in the 1930s.'

' "A paradox, a paradox. A most ingenious paradox." '

'Is that a riddle or something?'

'A quotation. From an opera.'

'And what exactly does it mean?'

'The great ironical paradox – your mother ardent for the Third Reich, Hitler and all that. Your father seeing history before it was written. "A paradox, a paradox, a most ingenious paradox." '

'A fatal paradox.'

Again he found himself listening to the small watery conversation of waves on the lake-shore below.

'I suppose in a way,' she said, 'I was the cause of it all. If I hadn't been coming it might, I suppose, have been simplified. I was the great complication. She was determined that England shouldn't have him. But Germany would.'

For some moments he sat in a state of bewildered disbelief, again listening to the waves talking on the shore, before asking at last if she was about to tell him that her mother had sold her father up the river.

'Not quite so crude as that. He just disappeared one day, in fact the very day war started. They found him a nice secluded little place in the country.'

'There are, of course, more ways of killing a cat,' he said, 'than choking it with custard.'

'Another riddle?'

'No.'

'Well, anyway, now you understand about hatred.'

Her voice was suddenly unbearably sad. And because of its new infinite sadness it also seemed to him impossibly, unbearably young. He was moved in consequence to put his arm round her and draw her head down to his shoulder. She let it remain there, in absolute silence, scarcely seeming to breathe, for ten minutes or so.

Finally, as if his thoughts about her unbearable youth had acted as a clue, she said:

'How old are you?'

His first answer was to brush his lips very tenderly against the side of her face; and then:

'Thirty-eight.'

She nodded. 'I thought that.'

'Something like half-way between you and your mother.'

To his infinite astonishment she suddenly turned full face to him, her lips confronting his own within an inch or two.

'Oh! no. Oh! no. You are much nearer to me. Much, much nearer.'

A moment later she was kissing him with such profound and prolonged passion that he found himself drowned and deaf in the summer darkness.

About ten o'clock the next morning he walked across the garden to the lakeside. Mrs Hauptman, as usual, was sketching under the stone pergola of vines, at the same time munching at the dark, sweet, perfumed grapes, skin, pip and all.

After an exchange of formal 'good mornings' he stood for a while looking over her shoulder, in silence, at the sketching pad. The drawing was again of the girl, but this time lying down, supine, in her sun-suit.

'Well, you don't say anything. Do you not approve?'

'It isn't as I see her.'

She laughed in her harsh German fashion. 'But that's hardly surprising. You are not I. Clearly I see things in her that you don't.'

'Clearly.'

'Perhaps she doesn't appear beautiful enough for you. What do they say? Beauty is in the eye of the beholder?'

'Perhaps ugliness is also in the eye of the beholder.'

She stiffened and had no answer. He stared again, in silence, at the drawing, unable to recognize in it a single feature of the girl he had watched in the sun-suit and had talked to late into the night.

'Isn't Trüdi down yet?' he said at last.

'I think she is still sleeping. She was very, very late last night.'

It wasn't difficult to divine that she knew of the previous night and he said:

'Yes, I know. We sat by the lake and talked a long time.'

'Very charming. And what lies did she tell you this time?'

'I'm afraid I must go now. I want to walk into town to get a newspaper.'

'Don't say I didn't warn you about that girl. She's a born liar. She started to tell lies in her cradle.'

'Really? The trouble with me is that I'm a born innocent. I've never been able to tell lies from truth.'

'With Trüdi it isn't necessary.'

He started to walk away. Suddenly she stopped sketching and called after him:

'The day before yesterday you promised to take me for a ride. Had you forgotten?'

'No, I hadn't forgotten.'

'What about this afternoon?'

'I'm afraid I can't this afternoon. I am going on a steamer trip.'

'Alone?'

Again it wasn't difficult to divine that she knew the answer.

'With Trüdi. It's the long one. It goes right to Stresa and Isola Bella and so on.'

'And doesn't get back till late. I know. I've been. You'll find it very boring by the end.'

The pointlessness of the conversation made him start to walk away again. And again she stopped him.

'I should like to see the dam again. You promised, remember?'

'I promised.'

'Then tomorrow?'

'Tomorrow.' He found it impossible to resist a parting shot at the stiffish erect figure now already sketching again. 'That is if I don't die of boredom on the steamer.'

'That, of course, is always possible.'

The steamer, white in the sun, had a marvellously tranquillizing effect on George Graham and the girl as it glided smoothly down the lake. Forests of Spanish chestnut, brown-gold, dark cypresses, oleanders in pink and red and cream drifted past and in between them lay villages of red and white and brown, themselves like clustered flotillas of boats moored at rest in the hot September afternoon.

'It's a good time for a glass of white wine,' George Graham

had said and for some long time they sat under a sun-awning on deck, drinking it, ice-cold.

'This hatred,' he said once, 'if it's so strong why do you go back to Germany?'

'I go to see my grandmother. She is one of the old school before the poison set in. She makes me an allowance. In fact it was she who sent me to England to be educated. She is the sweetest person – she lives in the Black Forest. It's very beautiful there. We go often to pick wild raspberries together. Oh! yes, I am capable of love too.'

'Did you think I doubted it? Did I ever say otherwise?'

'Please do, if you feel like it.' She laughed happily over the rim of her wine-glass, eyes sparkling like the cold white-green wine itself. 'Then I can give you a demonstration.'

'I shall put that in my notebook.'

She laughed again and the sound seemed to skip across the tranquil surface of the lake like a light stone playing at ducks-and-drakes.

On the way back, in the cool of the evening, they drank red wine, eating big fat ham rolls at the same time. No talk of hatred, love, jealousy or the past interrupted for a single moment the deepening gold of sunset, underneath which the lake turned from purest blue to dreaming opalescence and then at last to a calm dove grey.

'It will be dark,' he said once, 'by the time we get back.'

'Quite dark.'

'Too late for dinner.'

'Who cares? Let's have more wine. And more sandwiches. I'm still famished.'

As the day had dissolved into sunset his mind, and he thought perhaps hers too, gradually dissolved itself into a sort of after-bliss of wine. In due course he ordered another carafe of wine and, tasting it, said:

'My God, it's good. After a little while you get that mar-vellous feeling of what day is it and who cares?'

'Who cares? You're not sleepy?'

'Not really. Pleasantly soothed.'

She laughed again and he told himself, with some excitement, how much he liked her gay, wine-like laugh, the new expression of herself.

'I feel a tiny bit sleepy myself,' she said, 'I must confess.' She laughed yet again. 'Wouldn't that be funny – if we both dropped off. If we slept together on a steamer?'

The words made him reach out and touch her bare shoulder. The flesh was warm in the deepening darkness and he let his fingers move caressingly down from her shoulders. Gently she removed his hand.

'Not here. Not in public. There's a time and place for everything.'

It was very late when they finally got back to the hotel. In the card-room several groups of Germans were earnestly, sonorously playing bridge, devouring each other with suspicious, covert glances. On the terrace outside a few others were still drinking coffee. The night was still warm and the air full of the sweetness of hidden blossoms from some nearby tree.

'Like to walk by the lake tonight?' he said.

'Not tonight. Would it be greedy to ask for more wine?'

'Isn't greed one of the seven deadly sins? I can't imagine you guilty of any of those.'

She laughed again as he rang the wall-bell on the terrace for a waiter.

'You hear a lot about the seven deadly sins,' she said, 'what about the undeadly ones?'

'I didn't know there were any.'

'Perhaps there aren't. Let's have fun and invent some.'

'Fair enough. You start.'

'Love.'

'Yes. Love. I agree.'

'Sleep.'

'Sleep, yes, that's all right. I'm all for love and sleep. That's four.'

'Four? But you're doubling everything.'

'Perhaps I'm slightly tight. Any more?'

'The eternal triangle.'

'That, I think, is cheating.'

She laughed again and as she did so the waiter arrived with

yet another carafe of wine, red again. The waiter poured the wine. George Graham tasted it and passed it as good. Then he laughed again, infectiously.

'Cheers. I said I considered that cheating.'

'Why?'

'Because you can't divide a triangle into two, even an eternal one.'

'No? Perhaps we are not thinking of the same eternal triangle?'

She raised her glass to him, gazing at him over the red globe of it, with slow, soft, deliberate provocation. Then she sipped at it. The red moisture of wine lingered on her lips until she licked it away with her tongue and then he sipped too.

'Or are we?'

Her eyes, as she gazed at him once more over the rim of her glass, were extraordinarily limpid but crystalline in the lamplight of the terrace.

'Yes, I think perhaps, after all, we are.'

She suddenly stood up, at the same time picking up her glass and drinking.

'Well, here's to the first of the seven undeadly sins.'

'Love?'

'Yes, love.'

She gave him a long soft look and then picked up the carafe of wine.

'I'll take the carafe upstairs with me,' she said. 'Room 247. Tread softly.'

His dilemma next day was one of acutest agony. Daylight was breaking when at last he left Trüdi in her room and it was past eleven o'clock before he wandered into the garden. To his infinite relief no Mrs Hauptman sat sketching under the vines and then to his equally infinite dismay he found, as he was about to order himself coffee on the terrace, that she was sitting there, stiff and upright, as it might have been on sentry duty, waiting to challenge him for a pass word.

'You are very late this morning.'

The grass in the garden was wet. 'It must have rained in the night,' he said. 'I see there's a little snow on the mountains.'

'I hadn't noticed it.'

Drinking his coffee, he sat watching the fine high dusting of snow. Already the sun was shining and he knew that the snow would be gone by noon.

'You think it will be fine today?' she said.

'Oh! yes. The wind is right.'

'You haven't forgotten our trip?'

'I always keep my promises. It's my last chance to take you anyway.'

'Oh? And why is that?'

'I am leaving tomorrow.'

She stirred her coffee slowly for some time and in silence, her mouth thin.

'And where are you going? Back to England?'

'To Venice.'

Now he was silent too, aware that the moment of dilemma had come, was inexorable and couldn't be escaped.

'We are going together, Trüdi and I.'

She made a sound like an irate small dog snapping, perhaps, at a passing fly.

'I warned you against that girl. She started telling lies in her cradle.'

He paused and drew breath, heavily and with great deliberation.

'I happen to be in love with her.'

'Love? I warned you that she hasn't the vaguest idea of the meaning of the word.'

'I am in love with her.'

Again she made the aggressive sound, almost a snarl, of a snapping dog.

'In any case you are a good deal older than her.'

'You might also say that I am a good deal younger than you.'

'I despise that remark.'

For almost all of the remaining ten minutes of their being together on the terrace, toying with coffee, they hardly spoke a word. For her part there was no need. All evidence of her thoughts and emotions were magnified in her face: the excruciatingly tightened lips, the rigid chin, the opaque sightless eyes.

It was he who spoke at last.

'I hope this won't make you change your mind this afternoon? I am looking forward to seeing the dam myself again. It's the last chance I have.'

'Please say if you would rather go alone.'

'I am not going alone in any case. Trüdi is coming too.'

In a long pause he sat looking at the white fringes of snow on the mountains. Just perceptibly, he thought, the edges of them had begun to recede against the warmth of mid-morning sun. It was more than could be said of her voice, which when it came seemed to come from as far away as the mountain tops, and with equal frigidity.

'I will come. Shall I say I will be ready at half past two?'

Whether by accident or design he never knew, but it was almost three o'clock before she joined Trüdi and himself in the car. Her habitual regimental stiffness seemed to have increased since morning and she moved stiffly into the back seat of the car almost as if, he thought, she were a mourner at a funeral. In an attempt to counteract this he made what turned out to be a sad attempt at fabricating a jovial air.

'I thought the lunch was lousy today. Not fit for a cat. I hardly touched it. Mince and that disgusting *polenta*. I suggest we go straight to the top of the valley and gorge on that excellent local cheese. And wine. What do you say to wine, Trüdi?'

'I'm always ready for wine.'

He drove slowly up the steep curves and hairpins of the valley, past the burning chestnut woods, the dam, the stone bow-shaped bridge, an angler or two casting into the green-white waters of the stream.

'More water coming over the dam today. Must have rained or snowed more than I thought. We'll stop and look anyway as we come back. Are you afraid of heights, Trüdi?'

'Not in the least.'

'Your mother is.'

The remark, unanswered by either the girl or her mother, was as clear a signal for a newer, harder antagonism between them as if he had actually fired a rocket.

When they finally reached the head of the valley, neither woman having spoken a word, Trüdi shuddered as she left the car. At a height of only a thousand feet or more the air was suddenly chilled as ice.

'I'm sorry. I should have told you to bring a coat,' he said. 'Here, have my cardigan. I'm all right.'

He took off his green woollen cardigan and draped it round her shoulders. It might have been, from the distant tautness of the mother's face, that he had given her a bunch of roses.

In the *trattoria* Mrs Hauptman uttered only a single cryptic word in answer to his question as to what would she have?

'Coffee.'

'No need to ask Trüdi. Wine. And you must try the cheese, Trüdi. Marvellous. Will you have cheese, Mrs Hauptman?'

'Coffee.'

Soon it was clear that the air in the *trattoria* was as chilled as that outside. He made the bravest of attempts to thaw it, all unsuccessful.

'Have you ever been to Venice, Mrs Hauptman?'

'I have never been.'

'Trüdi has never been either. I've been once. It's magic. Pure magic. It was very hot when I was there and one day I was so overcome by the heat and the magic and all the rest of it that I almost fainted in the Accademia. An attendant had to bring me a chair.' He laughed in a further attempt to cheer things up. 'The weaker sex.'

There was however, no weakness in the stone-like silence with which Mrs Hauptman greeted his brief attempt at cheerfulness. It was Trüdi who made a deliberately uplifting remark.

'Take care you don't faint on me. Unless it's in a gondola. Then I won't mind.'

'Ah! the gondolas. The peace of it. You glide round dark narrow canals and then you hear parties in other gondolas –

singing, playing guitars, gaiety, sheer romance. No, that sounds wrong, romance. Ethereal, that's better. Can't really describe it, though. Anyway, you'll feel it when you get there. There's nothing like it in the world.'

It never occurred to him that these attempts to lighten the atmosphere were having on Mrs Hauptman an utterly opposite effect. It did not once strike him that raptures could constitute taunts, or romance a dark acidity.

Finally they were in the car again, driving back down the valley.

'We must stop at that funny little stone bridge. I want to get a picture of it. And then the dam. I want to get one or two of that as well.'

At the stone, bow-shaped bridge he stopped the car.

'I'd like to get a shot of the two of you on the bridge. Would you mind, Mrs Hauptman?'

'I am perfectly content to stay here.'

'But I'd like the two of you. You know – a sort of memento.'

There was no mistaking the peremptory bitterness of her laugh.

'Memento. You choose the strangest words. No: I am sure you will find Trüdi adequate.'

Presently he took a picture of Trüdi standing in the centre of the curved ancient stone bridge, alone.

'Funny. I felt a tiny bit dizzy as you were taking that. First time ever. Perhaps it's the wine.'

'Perhaps. Very strong, that wine.' He was in the centre of the bridge himself now and looked swiftly about him. 'I haven't kissed you today. Did you know?'

'I knew.'

'It was very beautiful last night.'

'Very beautiful. Very, very beautiful.'

'I'll kiss you now. Quickly.'

He kissed her quickly but softly, tremulously, and with great feeling.

'That was very beautiful too,' she said.

Back at the car it suddenly struck him that Mrs Hauptman

had the appearance of an animal behind the bars of a cage at a zoo, a frustrated tigress, imprisoned, negative of eye, held in a bondage not of her own making.

'Ah! well,' he said, 'now for a look at the dam. Quite an engineering feat, the dam. Quite beautiful too, in its way.'

Twenty minutes later they were at the dam and he was renewing the request he had made at the ancient stone bridge: he wanted a picture of the two of them standing at the wall high above the dam. This time, to his surprise, Mrs Hauptman agreed. It was rather stuffy in the car, she said; she would welcome a little air.

'The two of you walk along. I want to get half a dozen distant shots first. I think I'm running out of film, though. Anyway I'll finish this one on the long shots – it's in black and white anyway. I've got a colour one for you two.'

The girl and her mother walked along the high wall above the dam while George Graham walked the other way. A great white spume of water, much heavier than he had seen before, was pouring over the dam, creating its dancing mist of spray.

He finished the last of his black and white film and then, at the edge of the dam, as he walked back, paused to change it for a colour one. There was marvellous colour, he told himself, in the afternoon: a sky of purest limpid September blue, the faintest hint of lingering snow on the highest mountain tips, the burning chestnuts, the black cypresses, Mrs Hauptman in a plum-red costume, Trüdi in a yellow skirt with his dark green cardigan over her shoulders, the electrifying spume of whitest water falling from the dam. It was all perfect; it would all come out so beautifully.

A shriek like that of a hungry screaming gull cut through the air. He had a sudden impression of a salmon leaping half-way through the falling spume of water before realizing, a stunned moment later, that it was the falling body of the girl.

Mrs Hauptman stood rigid, regimented, alone on the bridge. Somewhere far below, the body of the girl was already lost from view and nothing remained now but the thundering falling waters, foaming onwards in their white frightening power.

The Man Who Loved Squirrels

The Man Who Loved Squirrels

Everybody called him Spile Jackson: perhaps because he spent most days of the year stripping and pointing chestnut poles for spiles and fences in a small triangular piece of woodland at the foot of a chalk gully half-way up a hillside. The hard road ended there.

He was a big man, bony-faced, a man of few words, fortyish, rather swarthy, with a mat of wiry uncombed black hair and massive arms hardened to the appearance of tree roots by long exposure to sun and wind and rain.

He moved for the most part in a slow cumbersome way, except when he was using bill-hook or axe. Then his touch was precise and delicate: as neat as a man trimming a matchstick with a razor blade.

Thirty or forty yards inside the wood he had built himself a shelter of chestnut poles roofed over with boughs and shavings of bark and floored a foot deep with chips and sawdust and curls of chestnut bark. This shelter was completely open on the south side and in winter and spring, before the boughs of oak and ash and hazel and chestnut thickened with leaf, he could work inside it and watch the sunlight, twenty yards or so away, flashing on the waters of a little stream.

In summer everything darkened over; he was shut away. The little shelter became swallowed up, a tattered hovel, unseen from the end of the road. Sunlight no longer penetrated to the open front of it. In the permanent summer shadow every fresh shaving of chestnut bark was a startling white curl, bleached as bone, as it fell from the pole.

It was perhaps this brooding shadow that gave the whites of his eyes a peculiarly bare and incisive brightness, so that they too looked as if made of bone.

Every day at noon his mother, a small, crisp, ferrety woman with hair like tangled sheep wool who always wore a pair of black old-fashioned high-buttoned boots, brought his dinner up to him in a square brown wicker basket.

It was the same basket his father had used, in the same way and in the same place, thirty or forty years before. Nothing had changed about it except the slip of osier cane that held the lid in place. Time had simply worn it down to the thinness of a knitting-needle and it had been replaced with another.

As soon as Spile saw her coming up the road he laid down his tools, put a match to an old-fashioned paraffin burner that stood on his bench and then went to wash his hands in the stream.

By the time he got back she was already in the shelter. She had by now turned up the paraffin wick to full and his stew of meat, onions, potatoes and carrots was heating on top of it. While she watched this, not speaking and sometimes giving it a sudden prod with a spoon, he opened a bottle of beer. The habit of having a glass to drink it from was one he never got into and he simply encircled the neck of the bottle with his mouth, sucking at it as at a large dribbling brown teat.

In summer she always brought him a couple of extra bottles of beer; sometimes three or four if the weather was very hot. Men with big frames like his needed plenty of solid food that would wear well, plenty of bread and potatoes and plenty of good beer to put their sweat back.

Sometimes at dinner-time he ate eight or ten good-sized potatoes. As she watched them disappear into the large soft-lipped mouth she could tell exactly from the expression of his eyes, which never appeared to change at all, whether she had brought him too many or not enough. She could always tell from his eyes, that were apparently so bone-like, so bleached and so inexpressive, what he was thinking. And perhaps next day she would bring him only five or six potatoes, or as many as ten or a dozen, according to the depth of hunger she saw there.

There were days, during the meal, when he hardly spoke a word. She was used to that. His father had also been a man of few words. She had grown used to long silences just as she had grown used to trudging up the road every day at noon, in all weathers, without ever questioning it.

But occasionally she managed to talk; perhaps she would say: 'Johnson's paid.'

That simply meant a little more to put by in the cash-box under the bed in her room at home and there was nothing he needed to say in answer.

Or perhaps she would say:

'Blackburn come asking about his spiles again. I told him they'd be ready Thursday.'

There was nothing he had to say in answer to that, either. Thursday was what he said; Thursday was what he meant. If he didn't mean Thursday he wouldn't say Thursday. He was a man of his word.

After his meat and potatoes there was either pudding or pastry to follow and after that he simply sat filling the bowl of a pipe with tobacco, pressing the shreds slowly and firmly down with a thumb that was like a big brown wooden spoon. He liked puddings; they wore well. He liked apple, plum or damson when the fruit could be got, or simply jam and treacle and sometimes dates in winter. He liked a pipe too.

As soon as he knocked the ashes out of the pipe she knew it was time to go. While he smoked she stared at the collar of his shirt, the bright eye of the stud that shone brassily in the collarless neck below the enormous Adam's apple, the big outspread thighs, the hobbed kip boots, the thick black cap that he always took off and laid aside when he was eating. Something, somewhere, would be needing a stitch or a patch very soon and accordingly she noted it.

She noted his hair too. It grew strongly, like dense black wool, curly in a wiry sort of way, into his neck and ears. It needed cutting pretty often; he needed to shave every day. The backs of his hands were hairy too and in summer, when he opened the shirt at the neck, his chest and neck were like a dense dark pelt without a trace of grey.

With this unblemished blackness of hair he did not look more than thirty-five: ten years younger than he was. The skin of his face and neck looked oak-stained. It was stretched as tight as leather. He looked completely content, unquarrelsome, un-perplexed, as if nothing could bowl him over. And the reason for this, she had long convinced herself, was because he had never had any truck with women. Women had never bothered him. And she didn't suppose, now, that they ever would.

He might have supposed it too as he stood in the shelter and watched her pick her way in her narrow high-buttoned boots through drifts of primroses and white anemones that covered all the floor of the woodland in March and April, or among the thick cover of bluebells and rose campion of April and May, or across the big papery tongues of chestnut leaves in November. Every day she took back with her a sack of shavings, a few white axe-chippings, for her fire; and sometimes, not content with that, she picked up a fallen oak branch or a bough or two of ash and carried them down the hill on her shoulder.

Watching her, axe poised over the block where he was point-ing spiles, he would tell himself she looked like a squirrel: greyish, nimble, darting through the undergrowth and down the road, brightly eager, hoarding things. Money under the bed, scraps of wool and cotton, buttons, useless bits of patchwork, sticks, axe-chips, shavings: everything had to be saved, nothing wasted, everything would come in useful, somewhere, some day.

And presently, in the quiet of the afternoon, squirrels actu-ally came down from trees and sat on the threshold of the shelter and looked at him. Nimble as his mother, fussing through the undergrowth of ash and hazel, they came to within a yard or two of his enormous feet to watch him, generally two or three of them, sometimes as many as five or six, small fore-hands playing about their mouths until finally he actually laughed and started to throw them scraps of cake and bread.

His pleasure at seeing them come down there to disturb his silence and share his food every afternoon not only showed itself in laughter. He actually started talking. He knew each of them by sight; some of them by name; he loved them all.

'Here, Greedy, drop that. Drop it, I tell you. Blackie, Blackie, come on Blackie. Not you, Woolly, not you. Here, Blackie, come on – look out, Blackie, here comes Ginger.'

He supposed there were scores of squirrels in that wood and

no two of them quite alike. All of them had their special ways. As a boy he remembered nothing but red ones, but they were gone now, all of them, and only the grey remained. But the one he called Ginger had a trace of rust down the back; Blackie was stained dark down the spine of the tail. The one he called Woolly had fur of cat-like, Angora lightness, fluffed as down in the slightest wind and there was another he called Pinkie, with rosy eyes.

A few years before there had also been an albino, a pure snow-white one, that always pranced like a nervous ghost among the highest branches, too timid ever to come down to join the rest. He had never seen it quite so often as the others and finally, after a winter and a summer, he missed it altogether.

He could only suppose that someone had shot it: some stranger, a trespasser, somebody who had no right to be there. That was the one and only thing that sometimes made him mad: people trespassing, traipsing in, breaking fences, tugging up bluebells, leaving the gate open.

They had no damn business there. He hated the sight of them. They had no right at all to poke their noses into his world.

On a hot afternoon in July he came struggling up the hillside with his horse and wagon and a big load of poles. It was always a long hard pull up the steep and narrow track and whenever he knew he would have a pretty heavy load up he always left the gate open so that the horse could get a long straight pull without a pause.

That afternoon, to his irritated surprise, the gate was shut.

He stopped the horse in the road. He unlatched the gate and slowly walked a dozen paces into the wood, listening. It was very quiet. Summer had enclosed and darkened everything over.

He walked as far as the shelter and stood first on the sunless threshold and then inside it, listening again. All his tools were in place. The paraffin burner and the filling can were on the bench, where they always were.

He listened for a minute longer. Then he thought he heard a sound of splashing from the stream. In full summer the water hardly ever splashed down like that, except after storms. The surrounding hills of chalk sucked up the rain too rapidly.

Over by the stream he stopped again, listening. Then he started to walk down the stream. Twenty yards away it widened to a shallow pool and beyond it a good bed of watercress grew.

On the bank of the pool a girl was sitting, back to him, washing her bare feet. Her legs above the shallow water, in shadow, were very white and he looked down at them with a still white stare, eyes as expressionless as bone.

'You know you ain't supposed to be in here, don't you?'

She turned her face sharply, looking up at him. Her hair was pale yellow. It was long and rather straggly and in the sunless air under the trees it was hard to tell how old she was – twenty-seven or twenty-eight, he thought, anyway old enough to know better.

'No?' she said.

'No.'

'Why not?'

She looked straight up at him. He stood in silence, staring back at her feet in the stream.

'I was just cooling my feet, that's all,' she said. 'Not before they needed it. I walked all the way up from Ashfield. Where's Hill Cross, by the way?'

As so often with his mother there was no need to answer. She was sitting on a folded grey coat. Her stockings, her handbag and her shoes were lying on the bank beside her. One of the shoes was turned on its side. It was powdered white with chalk dust and there was a crack across the sole.

'They said this was the road to Hill Cross,' she said. 'They said there was a bus up here.'

She pressed her outstretched feet against the bed of the stream, raising cloudy chalk mud that sailed greyly away in the shadow.

'It's always the way when you try to walk it. I got lost as soon as I missed that bus,' she said. 'Then the road stopped all of a sudden and I looked in at the hut to ask somebody – '

'You bin in there?'

'Only looked,' she said. 'Just looked.'

She turned her face away. The back of her neck was plump. Soft fair hair grew like down to the very beginning of her shoulders. A button had snapped at the back of the dress, at the top, clean as a half-moon, and was hanging by a thread.

For the second time she started pressing her feet against the bed of the stream. He resented the white-grey mud that was churned up, discolouring the water, and he said:

'You git out of here. I don't allow nobody in here.'

It was her turn not to answer. She stood up in the stream. She picked up the grey coat and slowly unfolded it and put it back on the bank. He saw then that she was tallish, rather big. Her limbs were firm and heavy, her hair very thick. It was only her eyes that, like her voice, were lively. They were quick and blue and small.

'If everybody – '

'I'm going, I'm going,' she said. 'Just tell me where Hill Cross is. Can I get to it up the hill or do I have to go back down there?'

For a moment she looked suddenly sullen, lips pouting. The lips too were rather big. The entire mouth was loose and red in the shadow as she turned and sat down on the folded grey coat and swung her legs out of the water.

He stood looking down. She opened her handbag and took out a small white handkerchief and started to dry her feet with it. The toes were soft, even and well-shaped. The nails were carefully trimmed. On the pure white skin little drops of water had collected like seeds.

'I said can I get to it up the hill?'

She was drying between her toes and he watched her almost without being aware of it, fascinated.

'What time is it? Must be four o'clock, mustn't it? I'd got to be there by three.'

Still staring, he started to answer her questions at one remove, not really thinking.

'Path'll take you up to the main road. About half a mile from there.'

'How far to the main road?'

He simply answered her earlier question:

'Quarter to four when I come up the lane.'

By this time she had finished drying her feet. Her legs had dried naturally in the warm air and now she simply ran her hands about them, smoothing away the last few patches of dampness.

He saw her white calves quiver as she touched them. She did not look up. Instead she searched in her handbag again and found her stockings.

'Must be a quarter past now,' she said. 'God, if it's that late I'll have to phone. Can't split this, I suppose, can you?'

She was holding the stockings in one hand and dangling a ten-shilling note in the air with the other.

'About a mile,' he said. 'Bit less.'

'This, I said. Split this.'

She held the ten-shilling note over her shoulder. He made a half-clumsy effort to take it but she let it go a moment too soon and it fluttered down to the bank of the stream.

'Here, careful with that,' she said, 'All I got in the world.'

She turned her head and smiled at him over her shoulder. It was the first time she had smiled. Her teeth, like her toes, were well-shaped, even and very white.

'Bet you don't believe me, do you? Honest, though.'

By the time he had picked up the note she had half-pulled on one of her stockings. As she rolled it up over her white thigh he started to feel in his pocket for change. Most days, working in the wood, he hardly carried a penny in his pocket. But on days when he bought poles he often carried ten or fifteen pounds on him, sometimes more. He liked to pay for poles as he fetched them; he liked to pay for things on the nail.

As she rolled up her second stocking she turned and looked over her shoulder just in time to see him fumbling with a bundle of notes and some silver.

'Anything'll do,' she said. 'Coppers though. Must have some coppers.'

She fixed the top of her second stocking to her suspender and pulled down her skirt.

'Know anybody named Gilbert up there? Mrs Robert Gilbert? House called Ferndown.'

'Can't do it,' he said. 'All I got is eight and five pence. Three half-crowns, sixpence and the coppers – '

She turned round on the grey coat, kneeling now, legs concealed, a black comb in her hands.

'My hair look a sight? How much did you say?'

'Gilbert?' he said. 'That's just after you get to Hill Cross. House on the right-hand side – '

'It'll be a local call anyway. I can do it from a box. How much did you say you could do?'

She had started to comb her hair. The yellow threads of it, smoothed out, ran like honey through the black teeth of the comb.

'Might have another copper or two in my jacket,' he said. 'It's on the truck.'

He turned as if to move away. Her hair had partially fallen across her eyes and forehead as she combed it. She threw it back now with a toss of her head.

'She said I was to phone if I couldn't get there by three. Fivepence did you say you had?'

'I might have another copper or two – '

'It won't be more than fivepence,' she said. 'Lend me the fivepence. That'll do.'

He simply stared. His eyes were bony, suspicious, defensive.

'Oh! Lord, don't worry, I'll pay you back. I'll get the note changed in the village. I'll walk back this way.'

She combed the last strand of her hair. He hurriedly pushed the notes into his pocket and then stood awkward and uneasy, the silver and coppers still in one hand while he scratched his dark forearm with the other.

'Don't think I'd let you down, do you?' she said.

She stood up on the grey coat. She turned her shoes over with her stockinged feet and started to slip them on. He watched her, still with nothing to say in answer.

'Blimey O'Reilly, just fivepence,' she said. 'Only fivepence.'

She stooped, not smiling now, to button her shoes.

'Good thing I trust *you*, though, isn't it?' she said.

'Me?'

'You put my ten-bob note back in your pocket.'

He flushed dark to the roots of his hair. He dived a hopelessly troubled hand into his trousers pocket and she stood up in time to see him staring at the red note he had folded in with the others.

'You'll ruin me, you will,' she said. Now she laughed again, teeth fully exposed, gleaming pure white in the shadow of the wood. 'But I'm ruined anyway, though. Never get that job now. Be five o'clock before I get there.'

'Job?'

It was again her turn not to answer. She picked the ten-shilling note from his outstretched hand. A pigeon started a soft continuous moan in a tree farther down the stream and over by the gate his horse rattled its bridle with a shudder in the hot still air.

'That's all right,' he said. 'You take it. You have it.'

He counted the five coppers into his right hand, holding them out.

'Mean it?' she said.

She might have been mocking him with the small quick blue eyes but he was watching her hands instead and failed to notice it. They were smooth, fleshy hands.

'It's all right,' he said. 'You take it.'

'Better have the sixpence too, hadn't I?' she said. 'Do you mind? In case it's more?'

'All right.'

'Thanks,' she said. The six coins, one silver, five copper, lay for a second or two in the palm of her hand. Then suddenly she shut her fingers over them and then smiled up at him. 'Thanks a lot. I won't forget. I won't let you down.'

A few minutes later he was standing by the gate, where his one and only horse stood fixed with glassy patience in the fringe of shadow that had crept across the track, and he was pointing out the way for her up the hillside.

'Be seeing you,' she said as she moved away. 'And a lot sooner than you think, perhaps, at that.'

He half-nodded, staring after her as she started to walk up the

track. At that time of year, at the height of summer, the thick
branches of hazel and blackthorn met completely overhead,
making a tunnel of leaves, completely shutting out the sky.

Half a minute later she was standing at the mouth of this
tunnel, turning to lift her hand.

'Elevenpence I owe you,' she called. 'Won't forget.'

She waved her hand. The long inner forearm was whiter than
peeled ash in the dense summer shadow.

He watched it, transfixed. It was the first time in all his life a
woman had ever lifted her hand to him and waved good-bye.

He was not very good at arithmetic. He was lost in a world of
calculation. Like his father before him he understood an axe, a
pole, and how they could be brought together. He knew the
fragmentary balance necessary to bring a blade against the tip
of an ash-pole and trim it as smooth as a pencil or a matchstick
sharpened with a razor. He was not very good at time either.
His mother was really the one for time and money and cal-
culations. She was the stickler.

That afternoon and evening his efforts at calculation gave the
girl half an hour to reach the house, half an hour there and half
an hour to come back again – he could safely say, he thought,
two hours in all. She would be back by seven.

In summer he generally knocked off by half-past seven,
sometimes earlier if he had the horse to fodder or work he
wanted to do in the garden down the road. He usually had a cup
of tea about half past four but that afternoon it was well past
five before he put the tea-can on the oil burner and walked
across to the stream to pick himself a bunch of watercress.

And there, to his surprise, over on the bank of the stream, he
found the grey coat lying where she had left it when she had
pulled on her stockings.

He picked the coat up and looked at it. One of the square
patch-pockets was partly torn away. The edges of the pockets
and the back of the collar were worn down to the bare thread
below the nap. One of the black-grey buttons was missing from

the front of the coat. Another had gone from the sleeve.

He slung the coat over his arm and took it back to the shelter. He hung it up over the bench and then, for half an hour or more, brooded over his tea. A fine white glare of late afternoon sunlight had begun to cut like acetylene light through an odd gap or two in the trees and wherever it fell it reminded him of the girl drying her white feet on the bank of the stream.

He was so bemused whenever he thought about this that he was presently unaware of automatically breaking off lumps of bread and butter and throwing them across the threshold of the hut for the squirrels to find. Later when three of them came to eat, and then a fourth, he broke up the rest of his bread and cake and watched them, bony eyes hardly moving, without a word.

A jingle of brass from the direction of the gateway brought him to his senses and made him remember the horse. He picked up a bucket and went back to the stream. He dipped water from the pool where the girl had sat, bathing her feet. The rim of the bucket caught the bed of the stream as he dipped and once again he stood watching the greyish churned particles of chalk clouding the water as they drifted away. Another shake of brasses from the horse woke his eyes to life again and suddenly he realized that every scrap of the chalk-bed had dispersed and settled again, leaving the water pure and clear.

It was nearly half-past eight when he got up on the truck, put the brake half on and let the horse start down the lane. For ten minutes or more before that he had stood by the gate, looking up through the tunnel of leaves, waiting and listening, but there was no sound except the moan of an occasional pigeon, a squirrel moving in the ash-boughs or a rabbit or two among the burnt primrose leaves and papery stalks of bluebell seed.

The sun had already disappeared by the time he was sitting in the kitchen.

'Wonder as the pudden ain't boiled dry,' his mother said.

'Had a bit o' trouble with a belly-band.'

'Oh? Took long enough to git it right then, din't it?' she said. 'I seed you go past at four.'

*

She was quick to look at his eyes when he had no answer, exactly as she was quick to notice the grey coat hanging above the bench the following day.

'What coat's that you got up there?'

'One I found in the lane,' he said. 'Hanging on a gate-post.'

He ate three or four potatoes without another word. She watched him in silence and it was not until he was filling his pipe that she went over to the bench and took the grey coat down.

'Ain't a mucher. Wouldn't do nobody much of a turn,' she said, 'would it?'

He had nothing to say in answer. She turned the coat round and round, looking at the lining and the buttons.

'Whoever she is she ain't much of a button-sewer. You can tell that.'

He was lighting his pipe now. He was pulling at it hard so that the upper edges of tobacco glowed in fierce red coils.

'When'd yu find it?'

'Yesterday afternoon.'

'Wadn't that kept you so late,' she said, 'was it?'

He pulled harder than ever at the pipe, not looking at her. The bowl of it glowed like the heart of a furnace in a smoky cloud.

She hung the coat back in its place.

'Nobody'll look for that,' she said. 'Somebody said good riddance to that all right.'

Before she could begin to pack up his dinner things he had the axe in his hand and was at the block, working.

'In 'urry, ain't you?' she said. 'You never finished your beer.'

'I got all day.'

The coat was still there next day, and the next, but she had nothing to say of it on either day.

On the third day, as she sat watching him eat his food, the sudden edge of a thunderstorm breaking over the hills brought rain rushing down through the woods in white, warm torrents. In half an hour the stream was gathering force down a saturated hillside, under dripping leaves.

'Don't soon let up,' she said, 'I s'll have to borrow that coat to git back home.'

Watching him, she spoke for once in a half-probing, half-joking way. He sat tense and silent, smoking his pipe, eyes not responding.

'Wouldn't keep much o' this out though,' she said, 'rate it's coming down.'

With the storm spreading slowly down the hillside the air had closed in almost dark under the roof of the shelter. Like a squirrel she rustled about among heaps of fallen shavings, fretful of the rain, fussing to be away.

'Ain't a bad lining though.'

She had actually taken the coat down again and was turning it over and over, then inside out, in her hands.

'Might keep me dry for that step or two,' she said. 'Keep the thickest on it out anyway.'

She raised the coat, opening it out, as if to put it on.

'Couldn't you sit still half a minute? It wouldn't hurt you, would it?' he said. 'Vapouring up and down.'

He did not often speak so many words at one time and she looked startled.

'Who's vapourin'?' she said. 'I got puddens to make. Hens to feed. Half acre o' washin' hangin' out.'

'Well, it's wet all right now, ain't it?'

After some seconds of silence he turned to see her actually draping the coat round her shoulders. It was several sizes too big for her. It draped about her like a cloak. The little grey head rose from the big loose collar in a ludicrous, maddening way. A moment later she moved her hands as if to button it up. He dropped the bill-hook he was holding. In two strides he was across the shelter, snatching the coat out of her hands.

'Leave the blame thing alone, I tell you!' he said. 'Leave it be. Leave it up there.'

'You want me to git wet through?'

'I got an old mac here,' he said. 'Put that on. Else put a bag over your shoulders.'

She stood silent. She had hardly ever heard him talk so much. She watched him hang up the coat above the bench and heard his voice sharp again as he turned.

'It's somebody's coat,' he said. 'Somebody'll come back for it. And if it ain't here when they come where do I stand?'

Before she could move or open her mouth he went on, still sharp but his voice slower now:

'Stealing by finding – police are on to you like grease lightning for a thing like that.'

'Sure they must be.'

She was watching his eyes, searching the bony whiteness for a clue, as she always did, to what he was thinking. But the whiteness seemed blanker than ever and now it baffled her.

'Don't want me to get in no trouble about it, do yer?' he said.

'No: I don't want you to get into no trouble.'

Ten minutes later a summer mist rising from a hot thin earth drenched by rain enfolded her grey figure as it went down the road. She had refused the mac and the bag for her shoulders. The rain was seeping down through the mist on to her bare head in a dead straight stream.

'There's wuss things 'n gittin' wet,' she said. 'I don't know as that'll hurt me.'

As he remembered it and stood watching her, axe in hand, he found himself half-calling after her.

'Knowing,' he said to himself. 'Knowing – cunning – that's what you are.'

A week later the girl was back again.

She came back on a Wednesday afternoon, soon after four o'clock, about the time when he usually sat feeding and talking to the squirrels, breaking bread and cake for them and sipping his tea.

'Back again, like a bad penny,' she said. 'Think I was never going to turn up?'

He was so slow in getting up from the box where he was sitting, all his big frame amazed, that she had actually finished counting out his money before he had taken a single step towards her.

'Elevenpence I owe you,' she said. She smiled as she held out the money in her hand. 'And cheap at the price.'

'You left your coat.'

'I know. The old rag. Always forgetting something – that's me all over.'

The day was warm and close. Harvest had started early that summer and farther down the valley a binder was cutting corn.

'Don't you want it?' she said.

'What?'

'Your elevenpence. Or do you want me to count it out for you?'

He laughed: neither very deep nor loud, but very much as if the sound were a break in a long-drawn sigh.

'I was thinking more about the coat,' he said.

He took the money, almost unconsciously, and put it in his pocket. She looked round the hut and saw the coat hanging above the bench, where he had always left it.

'About time I had another,' she said. 'Might do if I keep the job.'

'Job?'

'Didn't I tell you?' she said. 'Yes, I did. That's where I was going – that day you lent me the money for the phone call.'

'Up at Hill Cross?'

'You very nearly let me down,' she said. 'You didn't tell me there was an Upper and a Lower Hill Cross, did you? Two of them? That's how I got lost in the first place.'

'I – '

'That's all right,' she said. 'It all came out in the wash. Got the job on a month's trial. My first half day today – that's why I couldn't come down before.'

His tea was boiling on the paraffin burner.

'Is that tea?' she said. 'Do yourself well here, don't you?'

'I'll get another cup.'

'Here,' she said, 'didn't I say to you "Mrs Gilbert" when was here last week?'

'Think that's what you said.'

'Well, there's no Mrs Gilbert. Only a Mr Gilbert and a Miss

Gilbert. Two old birds. Miss is bedridden. Arthritis or something. I have to look after her and cook for the two of them.'

He poured tea into two cups, not looking at her. He took
bread and butter and cake from a biscuit tin and then closed the
tin and put the food on top.

'Where do we sit?' she said. Before he could answer she was
sitting on the floor, on a pile of dry chestnut shavings, her legs
stretched out. 'Arrived just in time, didn't I?'

Again before he could answer she bent her knees and started
to unbutton her shoes. She was wearing a grey-blue dress and
stockings now and he saw once again the level, well-shaped toes
quivering through the transparent flesh-coloured nylon as she
moved them up and down, relaxing.

'That's good. That's better,' she said. 'I've got awful tender
feet. They don't like these roads.'

He gave her a cup. She held it in both hands.

'Looking at my shoes?' she said. 'You might well too.'

He was not really aware of looking at her shoes and she said:
'Always hardest on the left one. Not that the other one's all
that much better.'

She picked the shoes up in one hand, turning them over,
showing two gaping cracks in the soles. In the left shoe the
leather was actually flapping loose.

'No wonder my feet hurt,' she said. 'I'll have to ask Miss if
he can spare an old pair she's done with.' She laughed. 'Would
you believe it? I have to call them "Miss" and "Sir". Strict
orders too.'

'I could mend 'em up a bit for you,' he said. 'I keep a last or
two down on the bench at home.'

'And what would I walk in while you were mending them?'
he said. 'Bare feet? They're my only pair.'

He could think of nothing to say in answer. She threw the
shoes aside, shrugging her shoulders again, holding the tea-cup
in both hands.

Then while she drank, he unconsciously began to break bread
into small pieces, as he did every afternoon, and throw it across
the threshold of the hut. At first, her face held close to the cup,
he took no notice of this.

'Ain't coming today, looks like,' he said.

'Who's not coming?' she said. 'Were you expecting somebody?'

'Squirrels.'

She turned her head sharply. She might have been seeing the quiet, simple, straightforward face, with its eyes of bone, for the first time.

'What squirrels?'

'They come every day,' he said, 'and have their teas with me.'

'They do? How many?'

Her questions were remarkably like the expression on her face: unsmiling but amused, incredulous but slightly mocking, as if she simply could not believe that a grown man could talk in that way.

'Three or four,' he said. 'Five or six some days.'

She sat quiet, gazing across the woodland. White cracks of sunlight broke the shadows without a flicker in places where trees had been thinned.

'Given you the go-by,' she said. 'Gone out to tea today.'

'Might be because you're here,' he said. 'They're quick on strangers.'

She checked a laugh, looking into her empty cup.

'They missed a good cup,' she said. 'I'll say that. Do they take sugar?'

The joke was lost on him.

'They only eat,' he said. 'Take bread and cake, that's all. What about you? I forgot to ask you. I was thinking about them all the time.'

Like his mother she seemed startled by the unexpected number of his words. He held out the biscuit tin. Then before she could move he suddenly remembered something and made a grunt of irritation.

'I'm all outa kilter today,' he said. 'Forget my head next. Forgot to get the watercress – '

He half-rose to his feet, as if to start off to the stream.

'Where are you going?'

'Off to the brook,' he said. 'It grows down there. You know – where you washed your feet.'

66

'That's an idea,' she said. 'If it was deeper I don't know that I wouldn't jump in altogether. My lord, it's hot. I could do with a bath – I get one bath a week up there. That's all. My allowance. One stingy bath. How about that?'

'You want some watercress?'

'I don't think so,' she said. 'That's "Miss", that is. She's the meany. One bath a week, that's her idea. And I'd hardly got that one started before "Sir" came hammering on the door, telling me how much hot water cost and was I going to soak there all night? She'd sent him. Can you imagine me lying there full length, having a real good soak, just getting my shape back after a hard day's work when all of a sudden I've got to drag my tired old carcass out?'

He sat listening, everything else forgotten. The very length of what she was saying mesmerized him. He stared deeply into the woodland. He could see really nothing in the tangle of summer light and shadow except the shape of her body lying in the bath, her white legs extended, and could hear nothing except the sound of a voice he did not know asking her how much she thought hot water cost and how long she thought she was going to lie here?

The voice and the meanness behind it angered him.

'Ah, some people, some people,' he said. 'All they think about is money. Eat and drink money. Money on the brain.'

'Ah! they're not bad,' she said. 'Might be worse. It's only "Miss", the old trout. "Sir" isn't too bad. He gave me half a tot of whisky one night.'

'*Half* a tot?'

'Half a tot is better than no tot at all, as the girl said.'

'What girl?'

'Oh! don't you know that one?' She laughed. 'Well, there was his girl and a – no – perhaps I shouldn't. Might shock you.'

Suddenly she looked round the hut, appraising it, as if really seeing that too for the first time.

'By the way,' she said. 'What do you do up here?'

'Spiles,' he said. 'Poles.'

'All the time? Nothing else?'

'All the time.'

'Not in winter?'

'Winter just the same.'

'You make a living out of that?'

'Have done up to now.'

By this time she had finished a second cup of tea. Now she sat with her knees crooked up, balancing the empty cup on the bridge they made.

'Surprised it pays,' she said. 'Just poles. Don't you ever get short of work?'

'Never have done yet.'

'Comes in steady?'

'Pretty fair. Did well in the war. Everybody did.'

'And spent it like rain, I'll bet. Everybody did.'

'Puzzle me. Don't see much of it to spend.'

'That's a poor game,' she said. 'Who gets it to spend? Ah! I know, wifey.'

'Mum takes care of it. I ain't married.'

As if wanting to make this small piece of information sound unimportant or trivial or offhand he started for the second time to break bread into small pieces and throw the scraps across the threshold of the hut. She waited for him to finish throwing the bread and then asked:

'What's she do with it? Tuck it away like the squirrels. I'll bet.'

'About it.'

'All work and no play for you,' she said. 'Don't think much of that.'

'I'm all right,' he said. 'I keep steady on. I'm happy.'

'Bet she is too.'

Suddenly she stood up and started to slip her feet into her shoes.

'Give me your cup if you've finished,' she said, 'and I'll go down to the brook and wash it up.'

'Oh! no. No. That's all right. Mum'll – she always – '

'Come on, give me the cup.'

'No. I'll do it. I'll come with you.'

'Oh! come on. Cup,' she said. 'A girl has to have an excuse some time, doesn't she?'

As he watched her pick her way through clumps of hazel, rustling with sloppy shoes through the papery stalks of bluebell seed, on earth dried as thin and white as slake lime by the heat of the summer, he found himself wondering if she would stop by the brook to bathe her feet again. For a few moments his mind rested on the picture of her as he had first seen her by the water, calves white in the shadow under the trees.

Then it returned to her shoes. For some reason it was impossible to explain he was oppressed with a nagging uneasiness, a certain sadness, about the shoes.

Nearly ten minutes later she came slowly back through the wood, carrying the two washed white cups. Now and then he noticed that she half-stopped and looked down into one of the cups, but it was not until she was actually in the hut again that he could see what was there.

'Look what I found,' she said.

'Wild strawberries,' he said. 'They grow up here on the chalk a lot. Thousands.'

'Have one?'

'You eat 'em.'

She poured the wild strawberries, about two dozen of them, into her hand. She started to pick them up one by one in her fingers and put them into her mouth. Then she laughed, her eyes brightening with the taste of them, and suddenly put her mouth to her hand, sucking them up in a single mouthful.

'Scrumptious. Marvellous.'

The berries, soft and dark and overripe with the heat of August, burst with brilliant juice on her lips. She laughed again, sucking at a drop or two of juice as it ran down her chin.

In a moment his handkerchief was out.

'Here, wipe it on mine,' he said. 'Save yours. It don't matter.'

'Thanks,' she said. 'Nothing worse than strawberry stain.'

The stain of strawberry juice and lipstick made crimson blotches on his handkerchief, almost as if her lips had been bleeding.

'What's the time?' she said. 'I must fly. Miss'll start creating.'

To his surprise it was nearly half past five.

'I'll get hung,' she said.

As she looked round the hut, hastily picking up her handbag from where she had left it on the bench, he found himself assailed for the second time by the sad uneasiness about her shoes.

'Look,' he said, 'about your shoes – '

'What about them?'

'I thought if you were coming this way again,' he said. Shyness spread a glaze across his eyes, leaving them bonier, whiter than ever. 'I could – well, I could bring the last up here – it wouldn't take long – I got the leather and things – I mend all ourn – '

'All right. What about Sunday?' she said. 'I get off Sundays.'

'All right,' he said. 'What time? Two o'clock?'

'Say four.'

He stood for some minutes watching her climb up the track white in its dark tunnel of hazel and blackthorn boughs, but it was not until some time after she had disappeared that he started shouting after her.

'Your coat!' he called. 'Your coat. You forgot your coat again.'

Two hundred yards or so up the hillside he caught sight of her leaning by a gate, resting after the steep climb, laughing to herself.

'Squirrels,' she was saying. 'If you can believe it. Squirrels. My God, squirrels.'

'You frightened them,' he said. 'They heard you coming.'

In the silence of the hazy, oppressive Sunday afternoon he sat feeding the squirrels when she came down the track, hatless, in a cheap short-sleeved peach-coloured dress, still wearing the shoes he had promised to mend.

'Sit down,' he said. 'No – not on the floor. Sit on the box. You'll spoil your dress.'

'My one and only,' she said. 'My Sunday best. Take a good look at it, You'll never see another one like this, I tell you.'

She lifted her arms slightly, showing off the dress for a moment or two before she sat down. He could see that everywhere the dress was a shade too small for her. It drew too tightly across her breasts and hips. It also seemed an inch or two short in the skirt. The short sleeves were creased skin-tight across the white upper arms.

'About time I had a new one,' she said. 'Some hope, though.'

'I brought the leather and stuff,' he said.

She started to kick off her shoes.

'Time they went to the rummage too,' she said. 'Or the rag-bag.'

Once again, as he took the shoes in his hands and started to strip off the worn soles, he was oppressed by uneasiness about them. It was bad that a girl should have to walk about in shoes like that.

'I'll do the best I can with 'em,' he said. 'They won't do you much longer, though.'

'Don't tell me.'

'This the only pair you got?'

'These and one more pair I keep for dancing.'

He tossed into his mouth a handful of tacks rather as she had tossed the handful of strawberries into hers. It kept him silent for some minutes as he sat with the iron last between his knees, paring the new sole to shape and tacking it down.

'Do you dance?' she said.

With the tacks in his mouth he was unable to speak and he simply shook his head.

'Never?'

He shook his head again.

'What? – you mean never? – really never?'

He shook his head again.

'Can't believe it,' she said. 'Can't believe you've never put your arms round a woman and had a flip round. That the truth? Really?'

He was glad of the tacks in his mouth. They saved him from telling her a still more incredible, more astonishing truth: that he had never even had a woman in his arms at all.

71

After that she sat quiet for some time, hands locked over one knee, rocking it slightly backwards and forwards as she watched him work at the shoes.

His own hands were muscular and hairy. They were good hands. It was only the nails, black and chipped, the cuticles split like celluloid, that gave them any sort of unsightliness and now she sat still longer in silence, staring at them, partly as if fascinated, partly as if wanting to trim them, file them down and clean the blackness away.

In this silence a solitary squirrel came down from the trees and started to nibble at the bread he had thrown across the threshold among the withered primrose roots and fallen leaves. She failed to see it at first. Sitting partly with her back to it, watching his hands, she was unaware of it crouching there like a small grey toy, nibbling at the bread held in front of its face, quivering, half-frightened, until it was joined by another, and then a third.

As he saw each of the three squirrels arrive one by one, out of the corner of his eye, he held his breath. He wanted to see how many would come down altogether and share the bread he had thrown. He was half afraid she would speak or move and frighten them away.

When suddenly she did move he shot out his hand quickly and touched her. His hand closed over the two hands locked across her knee. It was so sudden that she started violently.

Then she turned her head and saw the squirrels. They were seven or eight yards from where she was sitting. In the hazy afternoon, somewhere behind them, the stream was running so thinly after days of heat that it made no sound even when it fell over ledges of rock into the fields beyond.

Against this soundless background of haze the squirrels sat like little grey ghosts that had come out of graves, from haunts somewhere among the dead primrose roots, to play.

He knew that at the slightest breath of sound they would be gone and he sat feeling in his jacket pocket for another chunk or two of bread.

Finally he pressed a crust against her hand. She opened her fingers and took it. A second later she threw it, brushing her hand against the skirt of her dress so that it made a rustling sound. The bread fell short and a moment later every squirrel had gone, swallowed up in leaves.

'Oh, look! – there, I've frightened them.'

'They don't know you. That's all.'

She turned on him eyes wide with almost apologetic wonder.

'And I thought you were fooling!'

'Me? About what?'

'The squirrels. When you said the other day they came down and – '

'Didn't believe me?'

'I thought you were telling the tale,' she said. 'I've been told some good tales in my time.'

'Yes?'

'And believed them too.'

By the time he had finished the shoes he had also explained all about the squirrels: how they had been coming for years, how there had first been red ones, then only grey ones, and once the single, rare white one that he could only suppose someone had shot. He liked it when the young ones came. He was able to draw them slowly into his confidence until they were timid no longer and became his friends. He missed them on days when they didn't come. He missed them in the hard winters.

'How many do you suppose you've got here altogether?'

'Scores,' he said. 'Hundreds perhaps. No keepers here. Nobody to shoot 'em.'

'Don't they do harm?'

'No more 'n people.'

He turned the shoes over at last and let her see the new, clean soles.

'Best job I can make,' he said. 'Still, they'll do you for a week or two.'

'Week or two? They'll have to last me till I find a new pair hanging on the Christmas tree. What do I owe you for these?'

'Owe?'

'The ready,' she said. 'The do-ray-me, as they call it. These'd cost me ten bob at the snob's.'

'Don't owe me nothing.'

She smiled, blue eyes exceptionally friendly.

'Thanks. I won't forget that,' she said. She actually turned the shoes over and over, admiring them, saying how beautiful they were; and finally she touched his hand. 'I'll remember. I'll pay you back some day.'

'And if you want your dancing shoes doing I'll – '

'Dancing,' she said, laughing. 'I can't believe a grown man like you has never been dancing.'

The following day, when his mother sat in the shelter while he chewed in silence at his meat and many potatoes, she picked out with swift squirrel eyes a few scraps of leather, a few heads of tacks, that had fallen among the shavings of chestnut bark.

She looked too at the place where she had seen the grey coat hanging.

'Somebody bin for the coat?'

'Ah.'

'Who'd it belong to?'

'Gone when I got up here one morning.'

'Oh? Some gyppo I'll bet. Some diddecoy.'

She had noticed too the stains of crimson, strawberries and lipstick, on a handkerchief she had washed that morning. That was a strange thing, she thought; she was puzzled to account for that; then she noticed another thing.

'Don't your pipe draw no sense today?'

'Draws all right. Why?'

'You ain't smoking it.'

He neither answered nor looked at her.

She in turn fixed him with little nimble eyes that held him sharply, almost fiercely, in distrust.

'Time you got a padlock on this place,' she said. 'You never know who comes prowling about up here. Afore so long you'll start losing things.'

Every Wednesday and Sunday afternoon as the autumn went on, the girl walked down the chalk track to the woodland, always wearing one of the same two dresses, the grey-blue one on week-days, the cheap too-small, too-tight peach one on Sundays, and always the same pair of shoes.

He spoke once or twice of mending the dancing shoes and in turn she spoke again of dancing.

'Time to mend 'em when I get the chance to wear 'em out,' she said. 'Fat chance I'll get though.'

Sometimes she also spoke of 'Miss' and 'Sir': those meanies, those tyrants, those slave-drivers who kept her at it night and day, cooking, scrubbing, washing dishes, cleaning shoes, so gracious with their one bath a week, their few hours of freedom on Wednesday and Sunday afternoons.

This picture of her endlessly slaving for others moved him to angry discontent.

'Why do you stand for it?' he said. 'Why don't you get out and go?'

'Go?' she said. 'Go where— I'll bet you don't believe that was my last ten bob I showed you that afternoon.'

He confessed he'd never been able to believe it was.

'Cut my throat,' she said. 'Honest. That was my last ten bob.'

Before he could speak again she turned on him the wide blue eyes that were always so brilliant in the shadow of the wood and so lively and quick in comparison with his own and said:

'And to think I had eighty-seven quid saved up. All ready.'

'All ready? For what?'

'He took it. Walked out with every penny of it. Took all my clothes. All my shoes. Every stitch. Everything except that dress and the shoes I was wearing that day I left the coat here.'

'Who's he?'

'Fellow I was going to marry,' she said. 'Saved up for two years. Eighty-seven quid. I kept it under the bed. Like you told me your ma does.'

He pondered on these fresh acts of meanness and betrayal with growing antagonism together with a touch of pity.

'I bet you did a bit of wondering about me that day, didn't you?' she said. 'Wondered how I got myself into a state like that? Well – that was it. That's how it was.'

'Where'd he go?'

'Thin air. Did a bunk. He was sharp all right. Didn't call him Needle Johnson for nothing. He was a needle all right.'

She laughed, her voice unembittered but dry.

'I don't bear him any grudge though. What's the use? The money's gone – bet your life on that.'

'It was your money though.'

'I'll save up again. Take me a few years though. Squeeze twelve bob a week if I'm lucky. Take me a few years.'

Later, on a warm September Sunday afternoon, she suddenly stood up with a mixture of irritation and disgust, turning quickly round, showing off the too-tight peach-coloured dress in the brilliant lowering angle of sun.

'I'm getting pretty tired and ashamed of this dress though. Look at it. Look where I split it under the arm here this after-noon, putting it on.'

She raised her right arm. He saw the white underflesh of it naked as far as the shadow of the armpit. He saw the rip in the peach-coloured sleeve that she had hurriedly sewn up and the flesh pressing tighter than ever against the seam.

'Can't go on like this much longer. I'll bust out of it. How I'll get another I'm blessed if I know – but I got to get one soon, somehow.'

'How much'd new one cost?'

'Get one for four or five pounds,' she said. 'Perhaps three or four.'

'I'll lend you the money if you like.'

'Good lord. You don't mean it?'

Her hands sprang up to his face. 'You don't really mean it?'

'Mean it –yes. You say what you want.'

'Oh! I could kiss you. You're so nice I could kiss you.'

A moment later she did in fact kiss him. He was so dumb-founded by the sudden sensation of her mouth against his own that the kiss had prolonged itself for some time before she re-alized that he was still standing with arms dead loose, as if paralysed, at his sides.

Then she drew her mouth away. After that she took his hands and lifted his arms and steered them upwards as if he were a child being taught some simple elementary action for the first time.

'Put them round me,' she said. 'That's what I'm for. Go on. Put them round me.'

His hands groped about her body with strained timidity, trembling.

'Closer than that. I can't feel you.'

The big hands suddenly expanded themselves across the entire soft width of her back, feeling the dress smooth and tight as the skin underneath it. Then she laughed, putting her mouth up to his face a second time.

'That's better. That's a bit more like it. I can feel you now.'

When he spoke again his voice was choking.

'I'll bring the money Wednesday.'

After that she stood biting her lower lip in thought. For a second or two the pressure drew the blood away from it. Then he saw it racing and flushing back again.

'If you brought it Tuesday I might buy the dress Wednesday afternoon. If you didn't bring it till Wednesday I wouldn't be able to get the dress on Thursday because that's early closing day.'

'I'll bring it Tuesday,' he said. 'What time?'

'About ten o'clock. I could slip out then.'

It was past one o'clock on Tuesday night before he came down from the top of the hill, through the tunnel of blackthorn, now thick with ripening sloes, after seeing her home. She had kissed him over and over again in the shelter, lying with him on the heap of chestnut shavings, at the same time telling him how grateful she was, or how good he was or how understanding.

'What colour dress shall I buy?'

'Blue.'

'Why blue? Do you like blue all that much?'

In answer he spoke with solemn, direct simplicity.

'It matches your eyes.'

'I could have yellow to match my hair.'

77

'Blue,' he said. 'You have blue. It suits you.'

She laughed in the darkness, the laugh sharp and sudden, so that in the wood outside a bird, startled at roost, made a short flapping echo in answer.

'You always want your girls to wear blue?'

'You're the first one. Ever.'

'The first? Go on – *the first*? Don't believe you.'

He spoke again with that same painfully solemn simplicity.

'You said you'd never say that again,' he said. 'You said you'd always believe me.'

'Oh! I will. Promise. I'll always believe you.'

When he finally got home his mother was still in the kitchen, sitting at the table, under the lamplight, spectacles on, elbows pinning down a newspaper she had read through half a dozen times.

'Bin a-poachin' or summat?'

'More like after one. Like you said.'

'Pity you didn't take your gun then,' she said, 'and shoot whoever it was.'

'You're fast enough wanting to shoot people,' he said. 'You got to see 'em first.'

She didn't bother to look at him. With distrustful, squinting, microscopic eyes she stared at the newspaper, her voice level and cryptic.

'Don't allus need to see 'em,' she said, 'afore you know as they want shooting. Sometimes you can smell 'em a mile away.'

He never carried in his pockets, as a general rule, more than a handful of silver. He had not, on the whole, all that much use for money.

Whenever he needed money for chestnut or hay or oats or a new axe or to pay a bill or some sort he went to his mother. She in turn went to the box under the bed upstairs. He never went with her to the box; he had never cared very much what was in the box; he had never asked questions. She in turn didn't ask many questions either.

'Charge plenty for a few oats nowadays, don't they?' she might say, or perhaps: 'When one thing ain't going up I'll be blamed if another one is.'

But presently, as autumn came on, he began going upstairs to the box. Every Tuesday, and occasionally again on Saturday, his mother walked southward to the cross-roads and waited for a bus to take her to market. It didn't seem so very long, she sometimes thought, since she had travelled by carriers' cart, holding a big string bag in one hand and the baby on her knee. It took all day to go down to market in those days and half the night to come back again. You went round half the villages, delivering oil and seed potatoes and groceries and chicken in crate and chicken feed, and it was eight or nine o'clock at night before you got home by lamplight and took the baby upstairs to bed, still asleep in your arms.

On days when she went to market she always asked him:

'Coming back for dinner? Or shall I pack it and you take it up there?'

In the whole course of the year he came back to dinner perhaps half a dozen times. Except that the food never tasted quite so fresh he liked it better in the wood, alone, in the company of birds and squirrels, working away in his own time, in his own solitude.

That autumn he began coming home to dinner every Wednesday. When after a month or so she noticed this he suddenly changed his mind.

'Long drag down here and back again. I'll take it up with me.'

She always reached market by eleven o'clock and soon, every Wednesday, he was coming back to the box by noon. At first it was money for a pair of shoes. He was glad about that. There was nothing he wanted the girl to have so much as a decent pair of shoes. Then, as she herself said, it wasn't much use having a new dress and a decent, good-looking pair of shoes if your stockings looked as if they'd spent six weeks rolled up in the rag-bag. She was tired of looking as if she'd been drawn through a hedge backwards.

'Look at this pair. The damn colours don't even match: one

fawn and the other sky-blue-pink if you ever saw anything like it. I don't say my legs are perfect, but a good pair of stockings makes a difference. And it's getting too cold to go without any.'

That was always the trouble with clothes, she said; there was no end. You had to have shoes and stockings, then handbag and gloves, then scarf and hat if you wanted to look anyway decent at all.

'And another thing,' she said, 'you can't be all show on top and nothing underneath. Look at this slip. I've had it four years now, nearly five. Looks like a dish-cloth. Did you know I sleep in this slip? Did you know that? I haven't even got a night-gown.'

At first he took the money apprehensively, nervously, in small sums, not more than a pound or two at a time. Sometimes he simply asked for it, making ordinary plausible excuses.

'Chiesman says he got two thousand poles up there he wants to get rid of. Better get 'em in while the ground's dry. Better pay him while I'm at it an' all – he always looks in your hand afore you start talking.'

Presently the first few sharp snaps of October frost coloured hornbeams and maples a pure daffodil gold and soon sweet chestnut leaves were swimming down through the still air like slow shoals of brown-yellow fish, slapping against baring branches as they fell.

It was sharply cold on mornings of frost and sometimes he made himself a fire over which his mother sat while he ate at midday, rubbing her hands together like greyish slabs of pumice-stone, scratching the rough skin of the palms against each other.

'Got all your poles in? Don't look so many to me.'

'All there. Stacked 'em close this year.'

'See you did. About as close as Christmas is.'

All this time she was careful never to speak of money or his absences at night and on Sunday afternoons; nor of the lipstick stains on his handkerchief and the fact that sometimes he brought home two cups, washed clean.

But once she spoke suddenly of something entirely unexpected.

'Burn me if I didn't see a gal in that grey coat you had up here. Day afore yesterday.'

'Where? Up here?'

Startled, he was tricked into raising his head sharply before he was aware of it, so that his eyes were full-faced and naked for her to penetrate with her squinting stare.

'Down by the bus-stop. Biggish gal. Fair hair. Dyed I shouldn't wonder.'

'Never see nobody up here looking like that.'

'Never said you did, did I?'

He had nothing to say in answer; but it was enough for her to see the stunned blank eyes, bone-white as ever except for a faint flush of blood at the edges.

The girl too began to feel the autumn cold. She too began to sit over his fire on afternoons when the sun went down early and left a splintered, naked sky, cold and distilled, behind thinning yellow branches. And as she sat there rubbing her hands together, holding them out to the cracking chestnut flame and then drawing the white fingers of one hand slowly down the full length of the other, he could never help contrasting the sound and the look of them with his mother's stony, grating palms, harsh as a saw.

'My God, it starts to get cold.'

'You should wear your coat.'

'What coat?'

She laughed shortly.

'The coat you had. The grey coat. The one you left up here.'

'That!' she said. 'I sold that. Sold it to a second-hand place in Ashfield.'

He watched her shudder over the fire. He saw the skin of her bare arms pimpled with gooseflesh.

'Have to get something soon,' she said. 'Can't go on this way. No use – I'll have to slip down next Wednesday and get myself something. God knows what with, though.'

She watched him as he seemed to brood on this exactly as he had brooded in turn on the shoes, the stockings, the scarf, the handbag, the nightdress and the underclothes: partly in pain because he hated the thought of her going without them, partly in pleasure at the thought of giving the things she wanted.

He was quiet for such a length of time that presently two squirrels emerged from a clump of hornbeam and sat in front of the shelter, followed by a third and then a fourth a few minutes later.

Watching them, the girl sat with a smile on her face, brooding and dreaming too.

'You know what would be nice?' she said.

'What?'

'You know what I'd really like? What I've always wanted? Looking at them reminds me.'

He saw her staring at the squirrels that now, after several weeks, had begun to grow tamer and more used to her.

'A squirrel coat,' she said. 'That's what I've always longed for.'

There was no sign either in his face or his bony unmoving eyes that he had ever heard of a squirrel coat.

'Some hopes though,' she said. 'Some hope for a squirrel coat for this kid.'

'They cost much?'

'Terrify me to ask. Terrify me to think of asking.'

'How much?'

She begged him, with a sudden laugh, not to think of it. It terrified you to think of it. You might as well, she said, think of having diamond shoes.

'My God, though, they're warm. I'll bet they're warm.'

She sat clutching her shoulders with hands crossed over her chest.

'About how much?' he said.

'Oh! about a hundred. You could pay more I expect. Might pay less. I tell you I've always been terrified of asking.'

He had already started to brood on this stunning and impossible figure when suddenly he saw her jump to her feet, swinging her arms.

'Oh! let's forget about it. I just remembered something. There's a dance next Wednesday. What about going dancing?'

'No. Not me. I told you – '

Again she swung out her arms, laughing.

'I'll teach you. I'll bet you're quick learning. I'll teach you.'

'No, I could never – '

'I tell you there's nothing to it. I'll teach you – '

She gave another sudden laugh that drove the last of the squirrels back into hiding, quick and ghostly as ever.

'We'll go dancing. Have some fun. Hove a few drinks and have some fun. And I'll wear all my glad rags,' she said. 'All the things you bought me. All the things you've never seen.'

During the next three days he could think of nothing but the glad rags. His mind fermented constantly as it brooded on the glad rags. He wanted nothing else except to see her miraculously emerge from the chrysalis of shabbiness in which he had first seen her. What she would look like he couldn't remotely imagine.

And when finally he saw her he felt nothing but a shock of grievous disappointment. At first it shot through his confused head that she had turned up simply to have some sort of twisted fun with him, making him look a plain, simple stupid.

She arrived wearing an old soiled brown mackintosh with the belt and the collar both done up, although it was a mild evening without rain, and with an old green scarf, faded almost to colourlessness, tied over her head.

'Have a few drinks first?' she said. 'Shall we? It's early yet. The dance won't get worked up till ten.'

In the pub on top of the hill he drank thoughtlessly, stared at the mackintosh, which she never bothered to undo, and the messy colourless bag of a scarf that completely covered her blonde hair.

Several times she seemed amused by this stare. Once she laughed outright and started fingering the lapels of the dark blue serge suit he was wearing. It was his best suit; he had had it for twenty years. The cut of the lapels was high and old-fashioned. His white collar was narrow and stiff. A blue and white ready-made tie was fixed to it by elastic and under it he wore a thick blue-striped shirt.

'Got yourself up all right tonight, didn't you?' she said. 'No flies on you tonight.'

'I thought you were going to wear your things,' he said. 'Your glad rags.'

'Oh! You thought, did you?' she said. 'Well – you know what they say.'

'What?'

'You shouldn't think,' she said and once again she was laughing. 'It makes your brains tired.'

After this kind of talk he could do nothing but get his beer filled up again and then stare once more at the frowsy, incredible image of her wrapped in the dirty mackintosh.

'Well, if we're going to dance we'd better dance,' she said. 'The bar'll be closing in ten minutes anyway.'

'Want one more?'

The drink was a mere excuse; he was too shy to confess that he dreaded dancing.

'Not unless you do.'

'We'll have one more,' he said. 'Last chance we'll get.'

When he finally stumbled out with her into the street at closing time the October air was blowing cooler and he thought she huddled her shoulders still deeper into the mackintosh. And suddenly he found himself more than ever hating the mackintosh and dreading the dancing.

'Let's call the dance off,' he said. 'Let's go home.'

'Good God, no!' she said. 'The night's young. Only just beginning.'

'Yes, but – '

'I know,' she said, 'it's just because you've never danced before. Here, come here. I'll show you. Give me your hands. Like this, see.'

She started to show him, in the middle of the darkened village street, a few simple steps of dancing. He shuffled about the tarmac, tripping over her feet, and she laughed again.

'Loosen up,' she said. 'Let yourself go. That's all you got to do. Let yourself go. Heavens above, man, what's eating you?'

Ten minutes later he stood on the edge of the dance floor waiting for her to come out of the cloak-room. By this time he was so nervous that he was actually on the point of slipping out into the street again when he woke up from a beer-fuddled trance to see her standing beside him.

Slowly and stupidly he grasped that she was wearing the glad rags. She came towards him with outstretched arms bare to the shoulders. Her dress was silk, bright emerald green and cut low at the bust so that an inch or two of her breasts were showing. The skin of her breasts and arms was remarkably smooth and white and clear. Her shoulders were heavy and sloping and the whiteness of their flesh was sharpened because she was wearing a black lace scarf across them, narrow and thrown well back and falling away behind her arms.

'I had to wear that awful mackintosh because it was the only thing I'd got. I don't wonder you looked surprised.'

He was not only already long past surprise; he was long past any sensation whatever.

'Same with the scarf. Only thing I'd got and I didn't want to ruin my hair in case it rained. Do you like my hair?'

Her hair had been newly permed that afternoon into a mass of ringlets that folded close against each other like tight golden shells. He was dumbfounded by that too.

'Well, say something. You paid for it.'

'I think it's all right. Nice.'

'Thank you for it,' she said. 'You're awfully good to me. You know that? You're terribly good to me.'

He was not really aware of much else that happened that evening on the dance floor and he was still moving and thinking in a beer-fuddled and unbelieving sort of way when he found himself out in the street again, carrying the dirty mackintosh over one arm and holding the bare warm shoulders of the girl with the other.

'Well, this is me. This is where you leave me. Say "Good-night" to "Sir" and "Miss" – ' She laughed again. 'God bless them.'

They were standing in front of a large bay-windowed Edwardian house faced with red tiles and skirted with limes fre which big flat leaves were falling on to the street path outside.

'That's me. Right at the top. In the roof – right under the lightning conductor.'

He stood without saying anything, gazing up at her window.

'Not much of a room. Still, you can imagine me up there, can't you? Snug and asleep in bed. In my new night-gown.'

Every fall of leaf from the limes outside the house was like an echo of her voice dropping her words with quiet and careful separation.

'That's another thing you haven't seen yet. The night-gown. Nobody has. Except "Sir".'

'Except who?'

'Oh! he caught me going along the landing the other night and peeped at me. He's always peeping.'

He suddenly turned her body to him, trembling with jealousy.

'Peeping? Peeping? How? – how does that come about? – Peeping?'

'Oh! it's just his game. He's always at it. Trying the bathroom door. Knocking on my bedroom to ask if I want any letters posting. Thinks he'll catch me in the never-never. Take no notice of him.'

He found himself quivering, fired by improbable jealousies.

'If he does it many more times I'll tell him something though. And you know what? I'll tell him he can buy me a proper dressing-gown.'

'I can buy you a dressing-gown. I can buy you a dressing-gown.'

'Oh! let him buy it for a change. Let him spend a copper or two, the old skinny. They've got plenty. It's right what I said – they roll in it. I know. I saw a paying-in slip on "Sir's" desk the other day – paying into the bank. Two thousand odd.'

'They ain't the only ones with money,' he said. 'They ain't the only ones. I found out – '

'Found out what?'

'How much Mum's got. In the box. Under the bed.'

'All wrapped up in cotton-wool?'

'Over twelve hundred,' he said. 'In a brown paper parcel. I always thought it was just papers. Deeds or something. Twelve hundred or more.'

A breeze that lifted the limes had almost a sea-breath of warmth in it. Leaves dropped from the branches like a falling pack of cards. With a sudden odd detachment the girl lifted her face to a sky crowded with stars and said:

'Oh! it's too good a night to shut myself up in that box yet. Look at the stars. I'm going to walk part of the way back with you.'

As they walked back, arm in arm, she paused sometimes, looked up at the stars again and said how wonderful they were. She thanked him several times for a wonderful evening, for the drinks and for the dancing. She thanked him for the emerald dress, the black lace scarf, the new shoes and stockings and what had been done for her hair.

'And all the other things,' she said. 'All the underneath ones.'

Listening, he was almost unaware that they had reached the track going down to the wood between arches of blackthorn and hornbeam that were shedding, like the limes, a gentle and almost continuous shower of leaves.

'That beer made me thirsty,' she said. 'I tell you what. I'll come as far as the hut with you and you can make a fire and we'll have a cup of tea.'

Twenty minutes later she sat in the way she so often did, quiet, clasping her bridged knees in her arms, rocking slightly backwards and forwards, shoulders naked and rosy-white in the glow of the fire. When he had brewed the tea she sat with the cup half-balanced on her knees, staring over it at the sparking chestnut bark, her shoulders hunched forward, the neck of her dress falling forward like an opened purse.

He let the fire die down a little before saying, 'You said you'd show me your other things. You know, the – ' and in the pause as he searched for words she turned fully towards him where he sat crouching in her shadow. With her voice lowered she asked him what it was he wanted to see and while he was still search-ing for words a second time she lifted the hem of her dance dress and pulled down the lace edge of her slip five or six inches.

holding her hand underneath it so that the flesh of her palm shone through the filigree. 'It's just a skirt,' she told him, 'one of the new kind. Without a top. Do you like it? I bought a black one too, but I thought the pale green one was better with the dress. Can you see it's pale green? Can you see it in the light of the fire?'

'What else?' he said. 'What else?'

'There's nothing else you can see,' she started to say, 'unless –'

'Unless what?'

She drew her shoulders forwards again, hugging them together and nearer the warmth of the fire. It was getting colder, she said, they ought to make up the fire, but he was hardly listening as she reached out with her foot to push a branch towards the flames.

'What did you mean?' he said. 'Unless what?'

'Unless you'd like to see the shoes I bought. I've been carrying them all the time. They're gold. Did you notice? I put my old ones on for walking.'

'I saw the shoes,' he said. 'What did you mean just now? – unless? – '

'Unless I – '

She made a sudden pretence of shyness and drew his head down and started whispering in his ear.

'I'll make up the fire,' he said. 'You wouldn't feel all that cold, would you, if I made up the fire?'

'This is the time I need that squirrel coat,' she said. 'You remember the squirrel coat?'

Her bare shoulders turned and brushed against his throat. He was not even astonished to find them warm. A moment later he started to caress the soft underflesh of her arms, warm too, and she begged him to go gently, once again as if shy:

'That's me you're touching. Hadn't you better make up the fire?'

She was already half-lying down by the time he had piled fresh bark and branches on to the fire. Flame as bright as candlelight sprang from the crackling wood and shavings. The tips of her varnished nails gleamed as polished and scarlet as rose-hips as she stretched up her arms and said:

'Tell me how I looked tonight. How did you like me?'

His answer was so solemn and unexpected that she gave a laugh as he came forward and crouched down beside her.

'Not like that day you come up here first time, I know that. That afternoon you forgot your coat.'

'I looked a sight. Tell me. I know.'

'I felt sorry for you that day.'

All his first inexplicable uneasiness about her shoes, almost sadness, came rushing back. It was not within his power to tell her how wonderful, how unexpected or how transformed she had looked in the green dress, the black lace scarf and the gold shoes that matched her tight-curled hair. He could only say:

'I wouldn't want to see you like that again.'

A moment later he started to draw the dress from her shoulders, but suddenly she lifted her hands, keeping him away.

'How would I have looked in that squirrel coat, do you suppose? Instead of the mac?' she said. 'How would I have looked?'

The entire heap of fire was a dancing mass of candle-flames that seemed to be laughing.

'I'd like that coat,' she said. 'Buy me that coat. That squirrel one. Would you?'

She laughed again. She let him partially catch at her breasts.

'No,' she said. 'No – not until – '

His voice started choking. His throat was so constricted that he could hardly form his words.

'Anything,' he said. 'Anything you want. Anything – you only got to say.'

It was typical of his mother that she said, as she cooked his breakfast next morning: 'Somebody had a rare fire going up there on the hill last night. Wonder who that'd be? Shone in my window for hour or two. You see it?' and equally typical of him he had nothing to say in answer except:

'Off to market today?'

'No, I ain't,' she said. 'Not today.'

'It's Wednesday.'

'I know that. I got things to do here. I got the flues to clean out for one. The stove don't draw.'

'I allus clean the flues out, don't I?' he said. 'I'll do 'em tonight.'

'You're busy o' nights,' she said. 'I got plenty o' time.'

It was exactly as if she knew he was about to raid the cash-box. Her way of reading his thoughts through his eyes was a kind of second sight that made her say:

'You going down to Ashfield today?'

'What makes you think that?'

'Just thought you might be. Might bring me a dozen candles if you do. Turning colder, don't you think? It's a top-coat colder 'n yesterday.'

'I never noticed it,' he said.

It was cunning and crafty, he thought, the way she smelt things out. The fire, the box, the idea that he might go to Ashfield, the idea that it was a top-coat colder today: she was thinking inside him all the time.

In the afternoon he drove the wagon down to Ashfield, tied up the horse on the market place and started looking for a shop window showing furs. It was about four o'clock when he found one and in the darkening afternoon the lights were coming on.

'What would a squirrel coat be? How much?'

Well, the furrier said, a good Canadian squirrel, a nice one, that would be about two hundred pounds.

'Much as that?'

Well, the furrier said, you had to remember there would be about two hundred skins to a coat. Squirrels were small. Yes, all of two hundred skins.

'Many as that, eh?'

The furrier went on to say that he had a real beaute of a Canadian three-quarter squirrel just in. A real beaute. He could show it – no trouble at all.

'I'll drop in some other time.'

Then, half-way to the street he paused, thought for a second or two and slowly came back to give expression to a thought that had been eating at the edge of his mind ever since the night before.

'Nobody never brings no skins in, I'll lay, do they?' he said. 'I mean – '

For making up? the furrier said. You bet they did. All the time. Fox, badger, otter, sheep –

'Squirrels?'

Squirrel, everything, the lot. You'd be surprised what things he had to make up sometimes. Once he even had a dog.

'Tricky job, I'll lay?'

There, the furrier said, he'd put his finger on it. Tricky was the word. Stretching and drying the skin – that was the tricky part. If you didn't dry them right you had trouble. Most people nailed them up the wrong way round. Fur outwards. That was wrong. It had to be skin outwards. That way they kept for ever.

'Thanks, mister. I'll drop in one day when I'm this way again.'

'And don't shoot them,' the furrier said, laughing. 'That'll spoil everything. Put a bit of salt on their tails.'

On the way home he stopped at an ironmonger's to buy a dozen traps and before dusk on the following afternoon he was setting them about the wood. Bread was a good bait, he thought. They were used to that.

That day the weather was already mild again. In a sudden turn of wind the air was blowing from the west. It was a soft, uneven, capricious wind and the next morning it was blowing on the fur of his first dead squirrels, four of them, as they lay among the papery chestnut leaves.

If he had emotions of any kind as he skinned them, stretched the pelts and nailed them up to dry on the back wall of the shelter, his eyes had no way of expressing them. They remained infinitely static, bone-like as ever. At the same time a part of his mind unthinkingly repeated a catechism composed of nothing but numbers: four a day was twenty-eight a week, twenty-eight a week was over a hundred a month. In less than two months he'd have them all.

It never seemed to occur to him that this simple and inevitable arithmetic might somewhere break down. It never crossed his mind that the squirrels themselves might at some time give out, exterminated. The entire business was like the progress of night and day. One part followed another. The coat was the inevitable end. It had to be.

Over and above all he was determined to keep it secret. Solitude had made him a man essentially locked into himself, shut away. Now the greater part of himself was locked up even more securely, brooding on a dream that was really as vast as a mountain.

Presently, he hoped soon, the time would come to share it and that time would be a wonder. He saw himself on some not too distant day presenting his gift to the girl. In a big box was how he liked to imagine it, lined with coloured tissue paper.

With increasing regularity he also permitted himself the experience of seeing her face as it would be when she took the coat. He had no doubt it would be all joy. She would be crazy about it. It was the thing she wanted most in the world.

The skins stank a bit as they dried in the late November sun and there was a day when his mother, sniffing and peering about the shelter in her own ferrety way, said there must be a dead sheep laying round somewhere. She could smell something queer all the time.

'It's your nose then,' he said, 'that's all.'

'It's a sheep, I tell you. Else a rat. I'd find it and git rid on it if I were you afore I suffocated. I'll be blamed if I'd put up with a stink like that.'

'I don't smell nothing.'

'No? Stinks don't come from nothing. Something starts 'em. Else somebody.'

After that he moved the drying skins, forty-three of them now, to the far end of the wood, nailing the newest to a hurdle propped up against a tree and hanging the rest on a line, pegged there like washing.

'I notice you got rid o' the stink,' his mother said. 'What was it? A rat?'

'Yes,' he said. Cunning, that's what she was. Knowing and cunning. Why the hell didn't she leave him be? 'It poked its nose in where it didn't belong and got caught.'

92

'Well,' she said, 'it ain't the only one as is done that.'

Now and then the girl, half-teasing, half-reproachful, would remind him of the coat. In his utterly secretive fashion he had no sensible answer to give her except that once, in an exceptional moment, almost with humour, he told her that Christmas was coming.

'Christmas,' she said. 'Well, let's hope it won't be a white one. Otherwise I'll freeze to death.'

Then, on a calm, leafless Sunday afternoon in early December, she shocked him with a statement that struck him like a blow across the eyes.

'Well, it was a nice dream, that coat, while it lasted. I know I've had it now. Anyway I'll be gone in a day or two and – '

'Gone?'

'Going back home. Got a chance to start a little business with my mother if I can raise the do-ray-me. Sweets and tobacco. Plenty of profit in that.'

'You can't go!' he suddenly started shouting. 'You can't go now!'

'Here, here,' she said. 'Gently. I haven't gone yet. Who's doing all the shouting? I haven't got the money yet. Can't go without the money.'

Desperation actually blinded him for a moment or two, so that he was aware only of shouting incoherently at an empty wood.

She in turn was extraordinarily calm. She actually shrugged her shoulders, asking him, if he didn't mind, to look at it her way.

'I mean – I ask you. It's hardly enough to keep a dog alive, what they pay me up there. I mean, there's no future. If it wasn't for the roof over my head I'd have hopped it long ago. That and what you've done for me.'

'I'm getting you the coat,' he found himself saying. 'The squirrel one. It'll be a week or two – '

'Saving up?'

'Sort of,' he said. 'It'll be just a little while – '

'You're funny,' she said. 'You make me laugh sometimes.'

A second later entirely without thought, he made an astonish-

93

ing statement. He wished, he said, she'd come down the hill and
live with him and his mother.

'Two women in a house with one man?' she said. 'Not this
baby. Put your thinking cap on. The old lady wouldn't like it
much either, would she?'

'She don't like much I do at all.'

Which, the girl said, didn't surprise her.

'Why?' he said. 'How's that?'

He ought to take her out sometimes, that's why. Give her a
treat sometimes. How long, for instance, since he took her down
to market? He couldn't remember, could he? She betted it was
years.

'She wouldn't come if I asked her,' he said. 'She's like
that.'

Oh? Just let him try it. Let him take her out and buy her a
cup of coffee and a bun or something one day. Give her a little
treat. She was his mother, wasn't she? Didn't his conscience ever
trouble him about his mother?

If his conscience had never troubled him much about his
mother up to that time it began to trouble him increasingly as
the weeks went on. The squirrels started to trouble him too. The
smoothness of life as he had known it for years began suddenly
to disappear. Sometimes there were only one or two squirrels in
the morning traps; sometimes none at all. They were disap-
pearing fast; the few that remained were growing crafty.

His attempt to bring reasoning to all this only made him more
confused. And did she mean that about going away? All the
business about the sweet and tobacco shop? He didn't know;
but whenever he tried to bring some sort of reasoning to this
side of things he was a little more successful. She couldn't, he
knew, go away without money. So he'd be sure and take care of
that side of it. There'd be no more visits to the cash-box.

In his clumsy fashion he brooded on these things through the
rapidly shortening days, through misty windless afternoons in
which not even a ghost whisper of squirrels' feet broke the
wood's uncanny silences. By this time he had killed most of the
squirrels he knew by name. One by one the familiar faces had
disappeared and now there was no one to talk to any longer.

In his heart, by this time, he knew that he was never going to get the coat. The scheme was a dead failure. In spite of it he kept baiting the traps, setting them up and hoping. And all the time, in between the spells of hopefulness, he brooded, more than half helpless, wondering what to do.

Then, as he knocked off on an afternoon darkening early under a lid of slate-dark cloud he experienced what might have been an hallucination. He heard a sudden rustling in a branch of dead oak leaves, looked up and could have sworn he saw an unfamiliar squirrel: the white one, the old albino.

A moment later it disappeared; but not before it, too, had started to trouble him. It made him dreadfully uneasy, that quick, ghostly, unreal glimpse of it. In some way it haunted him. It might have been that it was the ghost of all the squirrels he had trapped, returned to torment him.

The next day he knew that it was no illusion. In broad day-light he saw it three times, twice in the morning and once, in the uncanny windless minutes just before twilight, in the afternoon. Its appearance, real enough but in some way ghostlier than ever, sent him brooding even deeper.

Quite suddenly he began to dislike the wood, even to be the slightest bit afraid of it. He was glad the next day was Sunday; he wouldn't have to come back up there on Sunday. He wouldn't have to be haunted for a day.

This uneasiness and a growing feeling of guilt oppressed him so much that he made a sudden attempt to appease his con-science by doing what the girl had half-flippantly suggested he should do.

Over tea that evening he startled his mother by saying:

'Thought I might drive you down to market Wednesday. Have a bit of dinner out for a change.'

She had never had a bit of dinner out for years. She couldn't for the life of her remember the last time and she was so as-tounded that she could only think there was some sort of catch in it.

'What's come over you all of a sudden?'

He wanted new boots, he said, a new belt and a few things. That was all. He thought they might go down together.

'Well, if I get the washing ironed and aired in plenty o' time I dessay I could git round to it.'

On Sunday he met the girl at the top of the chalk track beyond the wood and told her with a simple eagerness that seemed also to express a mountain of trust in her:

'Going to do like you said. Going to take the old lady out to market and have a bit o' dinner Wednesday.'

'Now you're talking. Now you're a good boy.'

His brooding had many channels but one of them troubled him more than all the rest.

'Not going away, are you?'

'Doubt it now,' she said. 'That scheme'll fall through, I think. Question of the do-ray-me.'

He wasn't half glad about that, he said. Terribly glad.

'See you Thursday then?'

'See you Thursday.' The next moment his arms were round her like a rope, agonizingly knotted, and his lips pressing hard against her forehead.

The next day he stopped setting the traps. He was suddenly frightened that he might catch the albino. He was uneasy that, if he killed it, it might be some sort of omen: a thing to bring him bad luck.

It was the albino, in fact, that finally destroyed his notion of having a coat made up from the skins of the squirrels he had killed and had once so often talked to. The idea was crazy anyway; it would be simpler and quicker, he told himself, to filch the money.

It was Monday when he decided this and it was late afternoon when he got to the house and he saw with great relief that his mother was at the foot of the garden, taking in washing. Two pairs of sheets obscured all of her from view except her legs and he slipped into the house without her knowing it.

Nevertheless he had hardly started to pull the box from under the bed when he heard her climbing the stairs. In that acutely suspicious way of hers she had somehow sensed his presence and as he came out of the bedroom, empty-handed, she was already half-way to the landing.

'Ferreting about for summat?' she said. 'What's a' matter?'

'Nothing. Nothing,' he said. 'Just going back up the hill, that's all.'

'Blamed funny way o' doing it,' she said. 'Be dark anyway afore you git there.'

'I got work to do,' he said. 'I can light the lamp.'

'Else a fire,' she said. 'Like you did Saturday.'

All of a sudden he felt impotent with anger and started to push past her on the stairs.

'Who is she?' she suddenly said. 'Who is she?'

'Don't talk to me about about my life. It's my own, see? My own. And I'll do what I like with it.'

'Oh? Take my advice and put a lock and key on it.'

'When I want your advice I'll bloody ask for it.'

'I daresay. I daresay.'

'And I'll tell you summat else. I'll damn well get my own back on you one day. God help me, I will. I promise you that.'

'Promise? Like the promise you made about taking me out for a bit o' dinner. Nothing much come o' that, did it?'

'I got things to do! I'm busy. I got things to do.'

'So I noticed. So I see.'

'I'll take you out one day, don't fret. I'll take you out one day.'

'Not now you won't. I'll take myself.'

'Mister Jackson?'

Three mornings later he was coming home with a heavy load of chestnut poles he had been to buy from a man named Williams over the far side of the hill. His horse was almost winded as it drew slowly up to the gate, which to his annoyance was shut. He thought at once of trespassers. He hated trespassers. But then it annoyed him still more when he actually saw a trespasser leaning against the upright beam of his shelter, smoking a cigarette: a man of thirty or so, in a duffle coat, sleek as a

The Man Who Loved Squirrels

ferret and with eyes of the same searching brightness and of a tobacco-brown colour, matching the smart trilby hat he was wearing, cocked slightly over his right ear.

'Stan' still.' His word of command to the horse was brusque and his manner as he walked across to the shelter was slightly hostile. 'You know you're trespassin'?'

'Sorry, mate. No harm meant.'

The trespasser blew smoke coolly.

'Summat I can do for you?' Spile Jackson said.

'Cigarette?' A smart silver cigarette case flashed in the morning air. 'Bit nippy this morning.'

'No, thanks. I never use 'em. Like a pipe.'

The trespasser helped himself to another cigarette and slowly, with cool deliberation, lit it from the first and then blew a long cloud of smoke, casually.

'I said summat I can do for you? Want some spiles or summat?'

'I saw your old lady. That is your old lady, ain't it – her in the cottage down the road?'

'That's her.'

'She said she didn't think you'd be all that long. I said I hoped not, because I'd got urgent bit o' business with you.'

'Urgent bit of – What sort o' business.'

'Well, I tell you.' The trespasser drew deeply at the cigarette, inhaled and then blew smoke in a series of slow, calculated clouds. 'It's like this.'

Growing more hostile every second, Spile Jackson waited some moments before speaking.

'Business? Wi' me? I never seen you before in my life.'

'No, but you been seeing my wife, haven't you?'

'*Your who?*'

'Wife, mate. The old trouble-and-strife. Don't tell me you forgot her already.'

Even in the already chill morning air, sharp from an easterly wind. Spile Jackson felt himself go colder.

'Yeh, that's her. Wife. Been buying her clothes too, I hear. That right?'

The line of Spile Jackson's mouth hardened, looking like the dark scar of an old wound.

'Fur coat an' all, eh? Musta cost a tidy few nicker, that, Canadian squirrel.'

'I – '

'Oh! I seen it, mate, I seen it. Congratulations. Very good taste. Very nice.'

'She never said she was married.'

'Couple of hundred nicker I'd say. So she never told you? Bit careless. Well, I expect it slipped her mind.'

'How do I know – '

'Well, I don't carry the old marriage lines about with me, mate, if that's what you mean. But take it from me, she's spliced to me all right. And has been for ten year and more.'

The trespasser knocked ash from the end of his cigarette with the tip of his little finger.

'Fur coat, night-dresses, party frock, undies, stockings – you must be made o' money, mate. Or else you got some plan.'

'Plan?'

'Don't you know there's a word for this sort of thing? No? Enticement.'

Spile Jackson was silent. His vocabulary did not include the word enticement.

'Yeh, that's it. Enticement. See, a bloke's wife is his property. Just like his house or his car or what have you. So if another bloke entices her away from him it's sort of stealing like. See? You get the old trouble-and-strife nicked, so you're entitled to damages.'

'Damages?'

'Damages, mate. The old do-ray-me. You take the wife-snatcher to court, all legal like, and he's got to cough up, see? How much? Well, depends on what the court thinks. Smart bit o' stuff, good cook an' all that – they might say a thousand. Perhaps only five hundred. Perhaps more.'

Spile Jackson simply stood staring at the earth.

'Course it's better if it don't go to court. I mean you got solicitors' fees an' all that. They soon mount up. So if it gets to court it's liable to be all that much tougher on the old pocket. See? Better to keep it outa court. Settle it private like.'

The trespasser again took out his silver cigarette case and

again lit a cigarette from the glowing end of another.

'You likely to be here tomorrow?'

'I might be.'

'Only I tell you for why. She's coming back home with me the day after tomorrow.'

'Home? Where's that?'

'London. Mile End Road.' The trespasser actually laughed. 'Don't look so worried, mate. Nothing to worry about. I'm not the mean sort. Fact is I'd let you off light. I reckon she's worth a thousand. But I'm easy. I'll settle for five hundred.'

Again Spile Jackson did nothing but stare down at the earth.

'Well, gotta go now, mate. See you tomorrow? Same time, sort of? Good. Then we can settle it.' The trespasser actually laughed again. 'Cheery-bye.'

For a very long time Spile Jackson stood staring at the earth. He was thinking of the glad rags, of dancing and the light of a fire in the night. He was thinking of feet in the water of a summer stream. He was thinking of the fur coat and how the naked body underneath it had been sometimes warm, sometimes cold. He was thinking too of the squirrels, all the dead squirrels, the squirrels that were there no longer.

And now and then he also found himself thinking of the box under the bed.

Next morning, as usual, he started to work, cutting spiles. But soon the hand that held the axe and was commonly so precisely accurate with it started quavering as if with a sort of palsy and he found himself fumbling stroke after stroke with it.

After a time, about half-past ten, he gave it up and started walking. He walked slowly up the track to where, at the extreme crest of the hill, it joined the main hard road running east to west. He walked eastwards. Half a mile farther on he came to the pub where, as it seemed, a life-time ago, he and the girl had had drinks together and she, gay with sudden life, had taught him a few steps of dancing in the street outside.

He went into the bar.

'Mild and bitter.' He paused. 'No, I won't. Make it whisky.'

It wasn't often that he drank whisky. But today the inside of himself was a quavering husk, dry and cold and bloodlessly empty. When the whisky had driven a spear of warmth into this husk he ordered a second and then, warmed still further, a third. A moment or two of indecision about a fourth was finally ended by his saying:

'Better make it a double. I can't get myself more'n half bloody warm this morning somehow.'

As he staggered back down the track, through the leafless wood, his head felt fiery. Once he paused and struck his hand with great force against the trunk of a beech, as if it were an adversary he hated and, like the girl and the trespasser, was responsible for all the complicated agonies of his being cheated.

It was almost midday when he arrived at his triangular piece of woodland. The gate was shut. The trespasser, sitting on a chopping block, was coolly, serenely smoking.

'Morning, morning. Nice morning. Nippy again though.'

Spile Jackson's axe lay where he had dropped it, a yard or two from the chopping block. He picked it up, at the same time staggering slightly, and across the trespasser's face whipped a flash of fear. It disappeared at once when Spile Jackson threw the axe into the shelter.

'Began to think you was never coming. I waited an hour or more and then I thought you must be down at the cottage. So I went down and your old lady was there. She was in a rare old two-an'-eight.'

'Two-an'-eight?'

'All of a tizz-was. Couldn't make head nor tail of her. Kept rabbiting on about calling the police – burglars been in or something. Couldn't make sense of her.' The trespasser performed his favourite little act of lighting one cigarette from another, and then deeply, almost luxuriously, blew slow, heavy clouds of smoke. 'Thought any more about that little matter?'

'I thought about it.'

'Favourable, I hope?'

'I got the money.'

'Five hundred?'

'Five hundred.'

'And cheap at the price. Sensible man, sensible man.'

The money was in an old chocolate box in the shelter. Spile Jackson went to get it and then came back with the box in one hand his axe in the other. The whisky had given his normally bony eyes a wild look and once or twice he swung the axe like a club as he walked.

'Here, careful with that thing. You might do somebody a bit of harm with that.'

'Know what? I could cut a flea in half with that axe. Yeh, a flea.' The eyes flared with dangerous glints of light. 'Clean in half. Now here's your money. Now git off my place. Git off I tell you! Else you might be that flea.'

The trespasser grabbed the old chocolate box, made for the gate he had carefully closed and then, not bothering to open it, climbed swiftly over the top.

Spile Jackson waited for some ten minutes, alone, before picking up the axe. Then he opened the gate, shut it carefully behind him and started to walk, still staggering slightly, down the hill.

In the kitchen of the house his mother was making pastry, rolling it out on the table with a rolling pin. He said no word. She had nothing to say either and it was necessary to hit her only once with the axe, with ferocious accuracy, before she fell bloodily to the floor, the rolling pin clattering after her, bloody too.

After that he found an old newspaper and wrapped the axe in it. Then he started the walk in to town.

When he finally got to the police station he went in. The duty sergeant, busy at a desk with some papers, looked up and said:

'Morning sir. Something I can do for you?'

Spile Jackson paused for fully half a minute. The wild light in the eyes had died by now. The old dry, sightless bony look was back. His mouth was dry too.

'I just killed my mother,' he said at last. He laid the blood-stained axe, in its blood-stained newspaper, on the sergeant's ⸺. 'Could I have a drink of water?'

The Tiger Moth

The Tiger Moth

On that first meeting with her she looked, he thought, exactly like a moth: a brown moth, brown-haired, brown-eyed, wearing a plain brown shantung dress. Like a moth too she looked placid, innocuous, soft, rather sleepy, with no hint whatever of the moth's reputed capacity for corruption.

At the time he was a navigator on Lancaster bombers, half-way through his second tour. A stray piece of shrapnel had sliced his knee-cap on a flak-cursed night over Hamburg eight months before, causing him to limp a little. It also sometimes pained him considerably: not, as is often the case with old wounds, when the weather was damp and chilly but when it was humid, thundery or very hot.

This and the glazed weariness of his eyes made him look several years older than he was. Long constant night strain had also caused his mouth to grow thin. It was more like a badly-healed steel-cut scar on his face than a mouth: an old wound itself on a young body.

It was also a humid, hot, thundery night when he first saw her sitting on a bar stool as he limped into a pub called The Blue Boar, his leg paining him a little, some ten miles inland from the Norfolk coast. She appeared to be drinking, modestly and innocuously, what looked like gin-and-tonic and he in turn ordered from the landlady, Mrs Forbes, half a bitter. At that stage of the war beer was very liable to dry up late in the evening of a long hot day and he was unsurprised at Mrs Forbes' answer:

'Sorry, Mr Williamson, there isn't a drop left on the premises. I couldn't give a mouse a mouthful.'

'Blast, I've been drinking that half pint for the last hour or more.'

'Terribly sorry. I'll tell you what I've got though – two portions of cold salmon. Very nice. And cucumber. I held it back because I thought you and Mr Thomas might come in.'

'Mr Thomas is on duty. Well, it's some compensation. Anything in the way of wine to go with it?'

'All I've got is a Graves. It's fairly dry.'

'Good. I'll have half a bottle.'

'Sorry again, Mr Williamson. I've only bottles.'

'A bottle it shall be then. Meanwhile, if the gin hasn't run out I'll have a very large pink gin.'

Suddenly by a sort of sixth sense, he became aware that the woman in brown was intently listening. The placid moth-like body suddenly seemed alive with acutely raised antennae. He at once felt curiously uneasy. He was irritated by an impression that she wasn't merely listening, but that she was actually eavesdropping on his very thoughts.

For some minute or two longer she neither moved nor gave the slightest flicker of a glance in his direction. Then his pink gin came and as he lifted the glass, pursing his lips with some eagerness, she suddenly said:

'I'm afraid it's all my fault. I drank the last of the beer.'

'Very wise.'

'I wouldn't have done it if I'd have known you were that thirsty.'

'If you'd have listened hard you'd have heard my tongue panting.'

She laughed and the sound came from deep in her throat, belying for the first time her outward moth-like placidity.

Presently he was buying her another drink and as she raised her glass he said:

'You wouldn't, I take it, be averse to a little cold salmon?'

'Far from averse. Thank you.'

'And cucumber? I read a story once where someone said that when you eat cucumber there's a taste of spring in your mouth.'

She laughed again, deep from the throat.

'And also summer?'

'And also, I suppose, summer.'

After a fourth drink, Mrs Forbes disappeared into a room behind the bar, coming back after a minute or two to say:

'It's all ready now, Mr Williamson, if you are. You can have raspberries afterwards if you'd like. But no cream.'

'My favourite fruit. Good show.'

The window of the little back dining-room looked out on a field of oats, pink-stalked with approaching ripeness. As he slowly ate his salmon and drank his wine he found himself looking at it with a certain half-dreamy solemnity, knowing he would frequently recall it as an expression of some sort of sanity in a world crazy with flak and sour with glycol the next time he flew.

'Far away?' she said and he said yes, he was far away.

It was typical of her, as he later was to discover, not to ask where.

'Well, not too far,' he said. 'Just the field of oats.'

And what was so special, she asked, about a field of oats?

'Hellish precious. Hard to explain.'

How did he mean? she said.

'When you do a lot of – Well, all I know is they're damn beautiful.'

She rested her fork on the edge of her plate and he noticed for the first time that she was wearing no wedding ring. He immediately changed the subject.

'Are you in one of the services?' he said.

No, she said, she was teaching literature and history in St Anne's High School for Girls. They had been evacuated from London to a mansion called Clifton Court. Did he know it?

'I see it from the air. Sounds pretty dull though. Still, fun and gossip in the common-room I've no doubt.'

No, she was free of all that, she said, thank God. She'd managed to buy a small cottage of her own.

'Sounds cosy. Perhaps I might invite myself over some time?'

'The garden's a mass of weeds.'

This enigmatic answer of hers had the effect of changing his interest into a certain excitement. Four pink gins and two or three glasses of wine had already given his vision some haziness and he now found himself looking at her rather as he had looked at the field of oats, seeing her with a distant rosiness.

'Cottage far away?'

About a mile down the road, she said.

'What about running you home? I've got a gallon of juice in the old banger.'

Well, she said, she wasn't sure about that –

'Don't tell me you're shy.'

Not exactly, she said, but she supposed it would sound stiffish or something if she said it was all so sudden?

'It has to be. Tomorrow night I'll most likely be on duty. And perhaps the night after that. Sorry if it sounds like the old line.'

She said nothing. A few moments later Mrs Forbes came to clear away the fish plates and cutlery and to bring in the raspberries in round blue willow-pattern dishes. There was just a dusting of sugar on the raspberries and they looked pretty against the blue.

'By the way,' he said, 'you haven't told me your name.'

'Craxton. Felicia Craxton.'

'Felicia. Uncommon name. I like that. Suits you.'

'Thank you.'

She gave him an idling, tantalizing smile.

'Feminine of Felix, I suppose. Felix, Felicia – no, perhaps better not pursue that. God, the raspberries are good.'

'Lovely and sharp after the fish.'

'No,' he said, looking deeply now into her dark brown eyes. 'You're much more like a moth.'

'A *what*?'

'Moth. A beautiful warm soft brown moth.'

'I don't know whether I should take that as a compliment or not.'

'Oh! compliment. Not the slightest doubt. Moths are beautiful.'

'Doesn't it say somewhere they also have a capacity for corruption?'

'All baloney.'

'And don't they have to beware of candle flames?'

'Not this candle.'

Throughout this conversation he became increasingly aware of a growing physical excitement. Impulsively he put out his hand to touch her right one as it lay face downwards on the table. And suddenly as if this were a signal, the door opened and an American voice said:

'Hullo, baby. The Forbsie said you was here. Sorry I'm late. Had to attend a court-martial.'

Williamson turned to see an American Air Force sergeant at the door, burly, rather fat of face, with signs of black stubble sprouting round a boar-like mouth.

'Court-martial? Not you. I hope?' she said in a voice incredibly cool.

'A buddy of mine, that's all.'

'And you baled him out.'

Whether the joke was intentional or not it was impossible to say but she laughed, the voice again coming deep from the throat. A second later, to his eternal astonishment, Williamson saw her get up from the table.

'I have to go now,' she said and again the voice was incredibly cool.

For some moments longer he sat impotently speechless before standing unsteadily up.

'That's my baby,' the sergeant said.

'Good-bye,' she said, 'thank you for the evening. I'm sorry, but this was fixed some time ago – '

Dumbly he watched her leave with the sergeant and then sat down, steaming with rage, and stared at her unfinished dish of rapsberries.

For a quarter of an hour longer he went through a twisted, furious dream, drinking the remainder of the wine, unable to believe that the evening had happened, that the innocuous, placid moth had been and flown.

At last he got up, more than a little drunk, and went back into the bar.

'Any brandy, Mrs Forbes? Any brandy? By God, a large one, please.'

He took the brandy back to the table. As he stared w

impotent rage at the oat-field in the late evening sunlight every head of it seemed to dance with mocking fire.

'God damn her,' he said, 'God blast her. God help her.'

For the next several days he went about in an agony of conflict, alternating between blistering hatred of her and equally searing anger at himself. Twice he flew on operations, once over Hamburg, once over Bremen, and each time it was the oatfield rather than she, the innocuous moth, that mocked him.

Eventually the weather broke and on a cool blustering wet evening he went back to the pub. There she again sat at the bar, again apparently placid, moth-like, innocuous-looking as ever.

'So,' he said, 'it's actually you.'

'Oh! hullo.'

'May I join you? That is, of course, if you're alone?'

'I am alone.'

Thanks to the cool rainy spell there was now beer in reasonable plenty and his leg gave no pain. He drank deep at a pint of bitter and said, his voice brittle:

'I wonder if Mrs Forbes has raspberries tonight? I know – or am I mistaken? – that you're fond of raspberries.'

The joke had been long thought out; but somehow it didn't seem very funny any more.

'Nor, I suppose,' he said, 'is there any salmon?'

'I'm afraid not.'

'The outlook is bleak.'

'Not, surely, as bleak as all that.'

He sipped silently at his beer.

Presently Mrs Forbes said from behind the bar:

'Will you be staying to eat tonight, Mr Williamson? I've got little – '

'No, not tonight, Mrs Forbes. I ate at the Mess. Thank you all the same.'

'I see. Would Mr Thomas be coming in?'

'I'm afraid not. Mr Thomas bought it yesterday.'

'Bought it? Bought what? Oh! I see – I'm terribly sorry.'

'Ours not to weep. It's just the way it is.'

For two minutes or more Felicia Craxton stared into her almost empty glass and then at last said:

'It's my turn to buy you a drink.'

'Thanks all the same. My cup is full.'

She drained the few remaining drops from her glass.

'Are you bitter because of Mr Thomas,' she said, 'or because of me?'

'I'm constitutionally bitter. It's my nature.'

'In that case I'll buy myself one.'

She bought herself a gin-and-lime. Rain beat heavily, almost like hail, on the windows outside. She was wearing a rather old faded mackintosh and she started fingering a little nervously at the collar.

'You're gloomy. I can only ask again is it because of me or because of – what was his name – Mr Thomas?'

'Mr Thomas, Maxie. Bad type.'

'If bad, why the gloom?'

'It's always the bad ones you miss most.'

'I don't really understand.'

Tensely, gloomily, he went on to try to enlighten her lack of understanding. Very bad type, Maxie. Whistled most of the time when not on ops. For ever unfaithful to the popsies. Born liar. Occupations: seduction, alpine-climbing and collecting shells. Cashed dud cheques, borrowed money right left and centre. None returned.

'Devious character.'

'I loved the bastard.' He laughed briefly, his voice brittle. 'Know what he'd do? We'd get him pickled after dinner in the Mess and then he'd do his alpine-climbing act. Along the picture rail. Edging along on his toes and finger-nails. Scaling the South Col and all that. All went well until one night he got to a length of picture rail that had merely been painted on.'

He laughed again. 'Bloody funny,' She was quiet.

'Collected shells ever since he was a kid. Holidays at the seaside, and all that. He always carried one as a mascot. Good-luck charm, sort of. Other types had a rabbit's foot or a St Chri·

topher or some other damn thing. He had this shell. Shaped like a cream horn – you know, the thing you get at confectioners.' He used to do rude things with it. Knew the Latin name for it too, but I'm damned if I can remember.'

His pent-up gloom had expressed itself in an unusual lot of words. He felt slightly less tense now.

'Damn funny thing. He was carrying the shell in his tunic pocket when he fell off the picture rail. Broke the end off. Upset him like hell. Went about for days in sack-cloth and ashes.'

'Had a sort of premonition perhaps?'

'You eat premonitions at this game. Three meals a day.'

Again she fingered at the collar of her faded mackintosh.

'Well,' she said, 'I suppose I really ought to go.'

'Another appointment no doubt.'

Her mouth tightened to a thin line that almost matched his own.

'You won't believe this,' she said, 'but that sergeant was in the middle of an exam at University when he was drafted. He's determined to graduate, war or no war, but he's a plain big dunce on English literature. Well, we happened to meet in the bar here one night and he told me about it and I offered to give him lessons three times a week. That's all.'

'Extra mural studies.' He laughed briefly again, not without a certain aridity. ' "Let me not to the marriage of true minds admit impediments." '

'I see that you, at least, know your Shakespeare.'

'An old love of mine.'

Now she started to button up the collar of her mackintosh.

'Well, I really must go. I've a pile of exercise books to mark before I go to bed.'

'I trust that one and all will get full marks.'

She stood up. The mackintosh collar was fully buttoned. Rain struck the windows with a heavier, quite savage attack.

'I will,' he said, 'run you home if you like.'

'Thank you.'

His ancient Austin, not much more than a pram, let rain through the roof. In the mile drive to the cottage a pool actually ʳmed in the lap of the mackintosh. He apologized and she said:

'I suppose you wouldn't care to come in for coffee?'

With icy brevity he merely said, 'Thank you.'

The fireplace of the cottage sitting-room was filled with pine cones. She murmured something about gathering them in the woods on her way home from school and should she light the fire? It would be more cheerful.

'Let me light it.'

'I'll start the coffee. There are lots more pine cones. They burn well.'

She went into the kitchen. He heard the clink of spoons in saucers. He put a match to the pine cones, which shot into flame almost explosively, burning with resinous sweetness.

'Will you have it with milk,' she called, 'or black?'

'Black, please.'

She came back into the sitting-room carrying a tray bearing two cups and saucers, a sugar basin and a small dish of biscuits. She had now removed the mackintosh, to be revealed wearing a scarlet blouse and a plain black skirt. The blouse, buttoned down the front, was cut rather low.

His idea had been to inflict some sort of revenge on her, quite how he didn't know, but suddenly the entire notion evaporated. As she set down the tray on a small circular table by the fireplace he suddenly noticed, to his intense astonishment, that she was wearing a wedding ring.

'I see you're wearing a ring tonight,' he said. *'Pour encourager les autres?'*

'I don't wear it at school, that's all.'

'Or, naturally, when you have dates with sergeants.'

Without a word she went back into the kitchen. Soon the aroma of coffee mingled with that of burning pine cones. Its effect was to excite him, so that when she finally came back with coffee-pot and milk jug he felt himself draw in his breath with involuntary sharpness. At the same time he got the impression that the light of the burning pine cones had ignited the scarlet blouse.

For some minutes they sipped coffee, not exchanging a word. During this time a strong tension built itself up, taut as the moment before a race starts. Finally he drained the last of hi coffee and set down the cup on the table and almost at the identical moment she did the same.

He turned to stare at her. It was in his mind to ask some questions about the wedding ring. When the moment came, however, he found it impossible to form the words.

For fully a minute the deep stare of the dark moth-brown eyes had him transfixed. Once her lips moved perceptibly, as if she were about to say something, but she stayed quiet too, merely letting her tongue pass slowly across her lips.

The gesture acted on him like an invitation. He moved forward to kiss her. A moment later, in an incredibly violent, almost tempestuous movement, she wound her arms completely round him. He was then sitting half on the edge of the couch, so that the strength of the embrace caught him off balance and a second later they rolled together to the floor.

They lay there together for fully five minutes or more, lips locked together, neither saying a word, until she actually helped him in the act of baring her breasts.

It was at last she who spoke first.

'I'm all for comfort in these matters,' she said. 'After all I have a bed.'

Some long time later he emerged from a daze, almost a coma, of half-exhaustion to see that the rain had stopped. The long twilight of double summer time had still not faded. The western sky was a great pool of orange-crimson, its reflection falling on her surprisingly large uplifted breasts with a tender glow.

After a time she said: 'I don't really think you believe me about the other night.'

'Never talk about the past.'

'Don't you want to know about my marriage either?'

' "Where ignorance is bliss" – '

'He was in the Army. His troopship was torpedoed somewhere in the Mediterranean. No survivors'.

'I'm sorry.'

'Well, there was a divorce pending anyway.'

He could find nothing to say but:

'God, I'll be glad when this bloody war is over.'

'Yes? It might mean I'd never see you again.'

'Do you want to see me again?'

She gave a great impulsive sigh, and at the same time swung her body round to face him.

'Make love to me once more. Please.'

Unshaven, taut, almost in a state of hypnosis, he eventually drove back to the Mess for breakfast and was then unable to eat it. Thereafter, for the remaining two months of the summer, except when operations made it impossible, he saw her night after night and sometimes in the afternoons. She was, she told him once, particularly addicted to things of an amorous sort in the afternoons. It was odd, but somehow it gave her a lovely feeling of guilt. That made it all the more exciting.

As for himself he spoke a lot of the future. Did she know what he longed for more than anything? Two things. He wanted to grow apples and buy himself a boat. Somewhere in the West Country. Something like thirty or forty acres. The boat a twenty-five footer. There was no sight in the world like an apple orchard in full blossom and no feeling like that you got when you saw a sail at full stretch in a good wind.

'No feeling? Not even with me?'

It was something like the same thing, he said. The curve of a sail or an apple always reminded him of the curve of a woman's breasts.

'Does that explain Adam and Eve or why men hanker after possessing boats?'

Could be, he said. But what did she feel? About the apples and the sailing, he meant. It didn't sound too impossibly dull for words?

'On the contrary.'

In due course he got a week-end's leave. They drove to the West Country, staying for two nights at a farmhouse as man and wife. Apples still glowed crimson in the October orchards. There was good rough cider to drink and home-cured bacon and home-baked bread for breakfast. The farmer had injured his spine in a fall from a hay-rick that summer and hobbled

115

about on two sticks. He seemed unlikely ever to work again, so that now the wife made a few pennies by taking in guests.

'Ever think of selling the farm?' Williamson said.

It wasn't a question of thinking, the wife said. If things didn't improve they'd have to.

'They say if you want a thing passionately enough you'll get it in the end. You name the price and I'll pay you a ten per cent deposit. The war won't last more than a few more months and the deposit'll keep you going that far.'

'We'll talk it over and let you know in the morning.'

Driving back east Williamson could only repeat, over and over again:

'It's a bloody miracle. It's a bloody miracle.'

'More like a dream.'

He loved her for saying that, he said. Well, it wouldn't be long now. A matter of a few months, he thought. The invasion had gone pretty well so far and for the life of him he didn't see how the Germans could last another winter. We were giving them hell with the bombing too.

'I'll be able to give up teaching. That'll be a relief.'

How she'd brightened up his war, he said. God, he could hardly wait for the peace.

Then at last came a day when he was obliged to tell her that his squadron was moving. He couldn't tell her where, of course, but only that he had just one more day.

In a long night of passionate farewell he again spoke a great deal of boats and apple blossom. She wouldn't let him down? God, he knew he kept on saying it – but it was all a miracle.

'More like a dream.'

No, no, he insisted, a miracle. His mind went back to the first meeting with her, his impression of an innocuous, moth-like quietness, and then the second, his almost suicidal bitterness about Maxie and then his final discovery that the moth, if it were moth at all, was at least, in its flaming affections, a tiger moth.

'You got me half-way back from the dead that night when I told you about Maxie. I loved that bastard. It may sound

116

screwy but I wanted to buy it too and be with him. Damn stupid, but that's the way it was.'

'I shall never forget your face.'

'You know what they say? – there's no future in it. But that night you got my future back for me. 'You *are* my future.'

'I'm glad.'

'And will be, for ever more?'

'For ever more.'

There eventually came a day when, the war finished at last, he drove his ancient Austin back past the grey distorted perimeter of the old bomber field, a kind of grass and concrete ghost town, and called for a brief drink at The Blue Boar before driving on to the cottage down the road. For some reason he found Mrs Forbes's manner uncannily quiet, guarded and withdrawn as she poured his gin-and-tonic. No, she wouldn't have one for herself, she said, thanking him all the same. She never drank in the mornings.

'God, I can hardly believe the damn war's over. Got myself a place down in the West Country, Mrs Forbes. Apple orchards. Near the coast. Going to get myself a boat, Going sailing every day. Fishing. Stuff myself with fish and apples and fresh air. How's that for a life, Mrs Forbes?'

'Sounds wonderful, sir.'

'Wonderful? It's a bloody miracle.'

Thus excited by both dream and future, he bought himself another gin-and-tonic, and then said:

'Mrs Craxton still around?'

'Oh! she's still around, sir. The school hasn't gone back to London yet.'

'Good show.'

He drove the ancient Austin down the lane towards the cottage. There seemed a threat of rain in the dull summer air. His leg, as it always did on occasions of humid, thundery weather, pained him a little.

As he drew up at the cottage he saw a tallish man in khaki army shirt and light khaki denims clipping, with a certain meticulous care, the top of a yew hedge. Behind him, in the garden, hung a line of washing, among it a black skirt and a scarlet blouse.

Williamson called from the car: 'Excuse me, sir, but does Mrs Craxton still live here?'

'Yes, she does.'

'Does she happen to be in?'

'Afraid not. Gone into King's Lynn to do some shopping.'

'Any idea when she'll be back?'

'Not till after lunch. She's having lunch there with some friends.'

Williamson was quiet. A few faint light beads of rain were now falling on the wind-screen of the car. He was suddenly conscious of a new growth of pain in his leg.

'Anything I can do? Any message or anything. I'm her husband.'

'No. Thanks all the same. No.'

'Garden's in a damn mess. Like a jungle. Take me six months to trim it into anything like decent shape. Spent the whole of my war in Cairo. Damn dull sometimes. But cushy, I suppose you could call it, cushy. Did you get around?'

'Here and there. Here and there.'

He drove the ancient Austin back up the road. Rain was falling faster now, leaving a tender sparkle on fields of young oats, on hedgerows breaking into an early summer miracle of elderflower, honeysuckle and wild rose.

The rainy air was very still. The oat-fields were also very beautiful and far above them, invisible in the gloom, skylarks were singing what seemed to be their endless, heart-breaking song.

Oh! Sweeter than the Berry

Oh! Sweeter than the Berry

Miss Shuttleworth, who much preferred to worship birds, and indeed animals, rather than God, believing them to be much nearer the Kingdom of Heaven, gazed with irritated dismay at a letter that had just arrived by the Friday afternoon post.

'The Reverend H. Sloane Arrowsmith will be calling on you at 8.30 p.m. on 16 July. If this is for some reason inconvenient to you he would be greatly obliged if you would let him know.'

'Hell,' Miss Shuttleworth said. 'The cheek. The confounded impudence. The old suet-head. Who in the name of sanity does he suppose I am?'

It further annoyed her that the letter had arrived in the middle of the highly essential task of bottling off and racking last year's elderberry wine, a task for which she had arrayed herself in a blue-and-white striped butcher's apron, her garden hat, a floppy red straw, and a heavy three-string row of scarlet glass beads. She was particularly pleased with the wine, which at not infrequent intervals she tasted. Beyond all doubt it promised to be of vintage quality. Clearly the long hot summer had put more than a little pep into the berries. Yes, she told herself as she tasted it yet again, this was the true, the blushful, the real McCoy.

Suddenly she found cause for even further, greater irritation.

'Holy grasshoppers and cockroaches,' she exclaimed aloud, 'the nut-head. Today *is* the 16th. Typical parsonic twittery. What a man. I always said his brain was covered with goose pimples.'

Her annoyance was now so great that for some moments she was quite incapable of further action. When she did move at last it was to look at the kitchen clock.

'Good grief! Twenty past eight already! I suppose I could

disappear. Yes, I could. I will. I'll lock up and go watercressing. Or mushrooming. Or some damn thing. Anything but that – that – Oh! in the name of John and Joshua I can't even find words.'

She had no sooner muttered all this aloud to herself than she looked out of the window and down the garden path. Tall hollyhocks, silken, in shades of pink and red and cream and yellow, lined the path on either side, the evening sun lighting up the many spires until they were positively lamplike.

Suddenly this ethereal summer picture was darkened by the figure of the Reverend H. Sloane Arrowsmith ('What a name, what a name,' she told herself), tall, black-habited, slightly stooping, looking very much like a pall-bearer suffering from acute dyspepsia.

'Great cod-fish,' she told herself, 'not even time to offer a blessed prayer.'

'Am I a little premature?'

He probably had been at that, Miss Shuttleworth told herself, betting at the same time that his mother must have been damn glad to get rid of the burden.

'The Misses Thompson were not at home. I'd allowed half an hour for them. Hence the slight dislocation of plan.'

It always struck Miss Shuttleworth that the voice of the Reverend H. Sloane Arrowsmith hadn't been oiled for a very long time. It grated, both on the nerves and on the teeth.

'You did of course expect me? This is a new idea of mine. You see I felt I ought to get a little closer to my family.'

Miss Shuttleworth sharply resented the idea of being part of a parsonic family so much that she was on the verge of choking. She managed to swallow hard instead and said:

'Of course, of course. Won't you come in?'

The dark, cadaverous figure of Mr H. Sloane Arrowsmith entered the low-ceiling kitchen, stooping still more.

'Ah, I see I've caught you in the middle of domestic tasks.'

'Wine. Last year's crop. Going to be the best vintage since '59. Have a drop?'

'Well, if you'll excuse me I think not. I had a cup of tea with old Mrs Sanders only an hour ago.'

Miss Shuttleworth couldn't think what on earth difference that made and at the same time urged the Reverend H. Sloane Arrowsmith to remember the Biblical injunctions 'take a little wine for thy stomach's sake', and 'Wine which makyth glad the heart of man'.

'That, I fear, is my trouble. It doesn't makyth glad in my case. It merely gives me chronic indigestion. Anyway I see you know your Bible.'

'Sucked on it. Took it in with me mum's milk. I can quote till the cows come home. Nice bits and dirty bits alike.'

'Which, if I may say so, makes it all the more extraordinary that we never see you in church.'

'There are other altars.'

The Reverend H. Sloane Arrowsmith, not quite understanding what this implied, looked puzzled.

'You mean you belong to some other faith?'

'Naturally. The faith of the sun, the sky, the moon, the earth and the waters under the earth. The fish, the butterflies, the foxes that have no holes and all the fowls of the air. "*And smalle fowles maken melodie and slepen all the nicht with open eye*".'

'That last quotation is surely not Biblical?'

'Not on your nelly. Chaucer. Great man Chaucer. So rich and earthy. I always thought I wouldn't have minded being Chaucer's lady-friend.' Miss Shuttleworth helped herself to another glass of elderberry, took a sublime swig at it and belched ever so slightly.

'You know,' she said, 'you really should try a drop of my wine. I have varieties other than elderberry. Red currant, white currant, parsnip, potato, lemon, orange, elderflower, blackberry. Golden Berry. May I tempt you?'

Successive glasses of elderberry had by this time brought a slight flush to Miss Shuttleworth's cheeks, so that she looked almost ready for the role of temptress. The Reverend H. Sloane Arrowsmith was, however, not immediately to be tempted.

'Golden Berries? I don't think I am familiar with them.'

'Cape Gooseberries. Those Chinese lantern things. Mr Shaw-cross up the road grows them for Covent Garden. Now and

123

then he has a surplus and brings me a box. Quite, quite superlative. You really must try a drop. I insist. I really insist.'

'Well, the merest modicum.'

What bloody silly language, Miss Shuttleworth told herself.
Typical parsonic bull.

She rose to fetch and pour out, into a tall thin glass, the
Golden Berry wine. It glowed with purest gold. She held the
glass to the light, so that even the Reverend H. Sloane Arrowsmith was moved to remark that it looked to be 'something
of a distillation'.

'Nectar,' Miss Shuttleworth assured him. 'Nectar. Purest
nectar. Those loaves and little fishes would have gone even
further with a drop of this. Come on, try it, drink up.'

The Reverend H. Sloane Arrowsmith drank up. His face too
glowed.

'Delicious. Quite delicious, I must say.'

'You know what I was thinking the other day? I mean about
these Golden Berries?' Miss Shuttleworth, like Pilate, did not
stay for answer. 'I was wondering why we don't have collective
names for fruits. After all we have a gaggle of geese, a skein
of swans, a murmuration of starlings, a pride of lions, a covey of
partridges and so on and so forth. Why not fruit? A plume
of plums, for example, a Corinth of currants, a perrydown of
pears. So for these Golden Berries. Why not a Guild of Golden
Berries?'

The Reverend H. Sloane Arrowsmith was familiar with the
fact that Miss Shuttleworth, with her downy moth-like appearance, was universally considered eccentric, if not plain
crazy, but this, it seemed to him, was rather much. Thus slightly
put off balance he was unprepared both for the fact that Miss
Shuttleworth was generously replenishing his glass and was at
the same time expanding her theory of collective names.

'And if for animals and birds and fruit why not for people?'
Miss Shuttleworth let out several light joyous peals of laughter.
'I thought some up. A licence of publicans. A lie of lawyers. A
mumbling of magistrates. A jaundice of judges. Like them?
Then a curry of curates and a boggle of bishops. But you know
the one I like best?'

No, the Reverend H. Sloane Arrowsmith confessed, he didn't.

'Well, drink up and I'll tell you.'

Mr Arrowsmith drank, slightly deeper than before – the very sweetness and gold of the wine was inducive to deeper sipping – and Miss Shuttleworth told him.

'A surplice of parsons! How's that? Short spell of inspiration, I thought. Got it late one night after three or four glasses of my red currant. Not only delicious but quite potent. Try some? Knock the Golden Berry back and I'll fetch a bottle of the red currant. It's got a certain something, a *je ne sais quoi* – '

'No, really, Miss Shuttleworth, really – '

'Bunkum. It's a source of inspiration – a positive candle to the soul. You'll probably compose the sermon of your life after it.'

The Reverend H. Sloane Arrowsmith wasn't sure if he needed a candle for his soul but there was no time in which to say so before Miss Shuttleworth was out of the room, gaily laughing, in search of a bottle of red currant.

'Hold that up to the light.' On her return she held the bottle up to the brilliant light of the evening sun. 'There's a beacon for you. There's nature showing her altar lamp. Worship in front of that – that's my motto.'

Miss Shuttleworth found a cork-screw and pulled the cork with the loudest of pops, smelt of it delicately and with a certain professional air and then proclaimed that you wouldn't find a better in the celestial spheres.

'Take a good slow draught of it. It needs treating with circumspection, if not reverence. I never made better. *In vino felicitas*, that's what I say, and this is *the* absolute *felicitas*.'

Miss Shuttleworth suddenly whirled the heavy three-string row of red glass beads round and round, as if to celebrate her triumph with the wine, so that it was as if the wine had leapt from the bottle and solidified into purest crystal scarlet drops.

'Like it? Approve? Find it good?'

The Reverend H. Sloane Arrowsmith confessed he did. Exceedingly good.

'Splendid. I'll let you have a few bottles for early communion.'

'Now steady, Miss Shuttleworth. I mustn't get all my communicants tipsy.'

'Why ever not? Splendid way to start the day. Come winter time I often have a good stiff swig of parsnip before I get to grips with my sausage and bacon.'

Miss Shuttleworth took a long deep draught of wine, at the same time urging Mr Arrowsmith to do likewise.

'I must say it strikes me as being a degree potent – I – I – ²

'I also make cherry brandy. None of your shop branded stuff but the real thing. Nothing but morello cherries, from my own garden, and V.S.O.P. Remy Martin. Splendid brandy. That'll warm up your gills.'

Several minutes later the Reverend H. Sloane Arrowsmith, who by this time felt that his gills had already been considerably warmed up, found himself amazingly acquiescing to a by no means miniature glass of cherry brandy. He was obliged to confess that that too had a degree of excellence. After several sips he felt, in fact, constrained to use the word superlative, which he repeated warmly, several times.

'By the way,' Miss Shuttleworth said, entirely and irrepressibly changing the subject, 'there was something I wanted to ask you. Of course I don't attend church service regularly but only at christenings, weddings and funerals. But tell me this. Why have you gone and mucked about with the Lord's Prayer?'

'But have we? I wasn't aware – '

'Appallingly and illogically balled it up.' Miss Shuttleworth fortified herself with a good deep draught of cherry brandy, at the same time taking the opportunity to replenish Mr Arrowsmith's glass. Mr Arrowsmith slightly pained by the thought that the church had mucked up the Lord's Prayer, hardly noticed and had no word of protest.

'Mucked it up. Good and proper. And shall I tell you how? You lot no longer say the most powerful and glorious words in it, do you? *For thine is the Kingdom the power and the glory.* Good grief, if the Kingdom isn't the power and the glory what in the name of all the saints is it? I reckon you've murdered the doxology.'

'Miss Shuttleworth, I think there are cogent reasons – '

'There'd better be. Good, solid, logical ones too. And do you use that appalling modern version of the New Testament?'

'Yes, we do.'

'Codswallop. Reads like a batch of Urban Council Minutes from the backwoods somewhere.'

'Miss Shuttleworth, I think perhaps I ought to be trotting along – '

'You know what that wretched version needs? A drop of this. A drop of wine in its shaky soul and bones.'

For a moment the Reverend H. Sloane Arrowsmith wasn't quite sure that his own soul and bones weren't the slightest bit shaky. The room seemed to spin ever so slightly. Miss Shuttleworth again twirled her beads and again they looked like drops of purest scarlet crystal.

'Oh! must you? But you must finish up your red currant and your brandy first. One simply can't waste nectar of that sort. Drink up, do.'

The Reverend H. Sloane Arrowsmith drank up. Ten minutes later he was making his way down the garden path, between the glowing silken hollyhocks, by no means steadfastly. Miss Shuttleworth went as far as the garden gate with him to say good-bye and he shook her effusively by the hand, at the same time saying how beautiful her garden looked, the hollyhocks especially. In answer she broke off a deep pink hollyhock and tucked it into his buttonhole.

He afterwards proceeded down the road in a certain state of more than slight confusion. A curry of curates, a boggle of bishops? A surplice of parsons? or was it a surplus of parsons? Either way he found it amusing. He even had a sneaking suspicion that it contained an element of mockery.

He paused to rest and reflect for a few moments by a field gate. He wasn't quite sure if Miss Shuttleworth needed prayer or if she was past praying for. He finally decided that she did indeed need prayer and that this was as good a moment as any to offer some.

Long experience had always insisted that he knelt for prayer. His knees wobbled. Faintly he sank down on them in the grass.

For some moments, eyes shut, he tried to find words of prayer to fit the illogical, eccentric, crazy character of Miss Shuttleworth, but nothing of a remotely original or appropriate nature came.

The only words he could think of, since by now he was feeling more than slightly dazed and sick, were 'Help her, Oh! Lord. Help her. For thine *is* the Kingdom, the power and the glory. For ever and ever –'

And as he said the words the hollyhock, pink as the setting sun, fell slowly, pure silk, from his buttonhole, and seemed to blossom in the grass.